THE LONGEST NIGHT

SAVAGE NORTH CHRONICLES BOOK TWO

BY LINDSEY POGUE

AN ENDING WORLD NOVEL

The Longest Night

A Savage North Prequel Novella
By Lindsey Pogue

Editing by Lauren McNerney
Proofreading by Letter-Eye Editing and Fresh as a Daisy Editing
Cover Design by We Got You Covered Book Design

Roar Press LLC
101 W. American Canyon Road, Ste. 508-262
American Canyon, CA 94503

978-1638481447

ONE
SOPHIE

DAY 1
DECEMBER 7

I'd just wanted to feel something for once. Was that really too much to ask for? Intense passion—an unbridled sense of all-consuming desire that fed my soul and made me feel alive. I wasn't dumb, I knew romance novels were meant to paint steamy portraits of ecstasy and lust, but I figured at least a fraction of that was possible. It's all I'd wanted—a tiny morsel of fiction—and my first time hadn't even come close. I wasn't sure I could even use the word *arousing*, or exciting, for that matter. The second time was the same. It was uncomfortable and awkward, and thinking back, I regretted every cringeworthy second of it.

I stared down at my journal, white pages open on my peach paisley-covered lap. *Worst decision EVER* was traced over and over across the top, beneath my poorly rendered sketch of a deformed Fabio look-alike, with shorter hair but an equally thick jaw.

Scribbling out his face, I flung myself back against my pillows. I'd never claimed to be a Michelangelo. I liked science and formulas, and tackling questions that held answers about the natural world, even if I had to wrack my brain to find them. Sex was my current problematic equation, one with two possible outcomes.

With a groan, I shut my journal, certain it was a bad idea to write down any of these particular woes and shoved it under my pillow as I turned onto my side. I gripped the edge of the mattress in my hand and exhaled the passing nausea, like I'd done throughout the night. I wasn't sure if it was a more permanent symptom of my boredom and stupidity or just my stressing out about the unknown at this point.

My room was dim and gray in the early morning light, which felt adequate given my mood. My body craved sleep, but my anxiety was calling the shots. I was too sick to my stomach to even close my eyes, let alone escape the impending possibilities of my future.

My mom slammed a cupboard door shut and the blender belched to life in the kitchen, making my skin crawl as I sank deeper into the mattress. The thought of eating or drinking anything made my insides lurch, and I groaned again.

I reached for my phone, charging on my side table. It was 7:00 a.m. and I still hadn't heard back from Jesse. For the hundredth time in eight hours, I checked my text messages to make sure they'd gone through. Everything about Whitely was unpredictable, especially cell phone service in the apartment complex during the winter. Whitely was one of many tiny Alaskan towns that didn't fare well during storm season.

Me: I need to talk to you. Call me ASAP.

Me: It's important Jesse. Call me!

Me: If you're playing your stupid video games, I swear to God . . .

Me: I'm late. Do you know what that means, idiot!!?? Like I-might-be-pregnant sort of late . . .

Me: Jesse, please call me. I'm seriously freaking out!

I met Jesse in middle school when I'd moved to town. He was

one of those boys that was smart and quiet, sometimes even sweet. But like most guys my age, his priorities were a bit skewed, and I often wondered if I wasn't more of an afterthought. Our graduation from friends to something more just sort of happened because we were hanging out so much; our parents and friends started to assume we were more together than we let on. In all honesty, Jesse was the best option I had in a town with only a dozen other people my age—most of them girls. My mom and his mom were friends, which meant he was "suitable" for me.

During our junior year we'd kissed, and now in the final stretch of senior year we were officially "an item"—according to my dad. But our relationship primarily consisted of us hanging out at the touristy ice cream shop on the pier, on the nights he didn't have earth saving missions to complete with his online gaming buddies. Most of the time, I was okay with that. I'd never thought Jesse was *the one* or anything, but I thought he was at least decent enough to text me back, especially if his life was potentially in danger. I wasn't sure who he'd need to be more afraid of if it turned out I was pregnant—my dad . . . or my mom.

I shoved my phone under my pillow with my journal, praying my cell would ding with a message notification, even if I got the sickening suspicion Jesse was ignoring me on purpose.

Of course he wasn't ready to be a dad, especially since his mom still made his sandwiches every day for his lunch. I wasn't ready to be a mom though, either, and not only might I be *pregnant*, but my boyfriend was blowing me off, and my best friend, Bailey, was on the East Coast, visiting her dying grandmother who'd caught a bad case of pneumonia and had yet to fully recover.

Unless I told my mom, which was the last thing on earth I wanted to do, I was alone in this. Freaking out and utterly alone. I nervously weighed my options.

Option one: walk into the only market, located in the only residential building in Whitely where *everyone* knew who I was—if only because of my mom—to have them witness what I was buying.

Option two: accompany my mom during her next trip into the city and try to sneak away long enough to make a quick purchase without her knowing.

I was hoping for a more appealing option three, but I could think of nothing.

"Sophie!" My mom's voice ricocheted through the apartment. I wondered if my neighbor, JJ, ever got tired of living next to the resident bullhorn.

Heaving out a breath, I stared up at the stark white ceiling, painted in inky shadows that filtered in through the cracked, blush-colored curtains that had been there since I was eleven. I could tell by the muffled silence outside that the snowfall had been heavy throughout the night. There were no gulls calling in the breeze, and the buoys dinging in the harbor were only audible if I held my breath to listen.

"Sophie!" she called again. Sometimes it was difficult to tell if she was using her mom voice or her mayor voice, like maybe she forgot she was talking to her daughter and not some city official she often came to verbal blows with. "You better be up . . ."

I had a dozen reasons to miss school, none of which I could tell my mom about. Exhaustion. Anxiety. *Morning sickness*. So I just lay there on the cusp of vomiting, my mind racing and dread settling deep into my bones as I prayed my mom was running late and would rush out the door without popping her head in to check on me.

"Your protein smoothie is on the counter!"

"Yum," I grumbled and pulled the covers up over my face. My stomach churned at the thought of the purple, overripe banana concoction waiting for consumption.

"Soph—why haven't I heard the shower yet?" My bedroom door opened, and I could almost feel the air in the room being sucked out as my mom inhaled an angry breath. "Sophie," she groused. Could other teenagers hear the frustration every time their parents simply said their name?

Her high heels clomped into my room as she tore the comforter off me. "What is this?" she chided, looming over me.

"I'm sick today."

She patted my hip. "Come on, get up." Her long, deep red-and-mocha hair was perfectly curled at the ends, looking almost black in the morning shadows. "A shower will make you feel better. School starts in thirty minutes, and you should be dressed already." Her favorite taupe pantsuit was perfectly pressed and her blue eyes were thinly etched with black liner. Nothing was out of place, everything was flawless and it was enough to make me finally puke, but I refrained.

"You were fine last night, Sophie."

"No, actually, I wasn't fine last night," I growled and pulled the covers back up around me. "I felt like crap, and since I couldn't sleep, I feel even worse."

She rested her hands on her hips, eyeing me closely. I was waiting for her to ask me if I was okay, allowing me the opportunity to give her a real answer, but instead she asked, "Are you and Jesse fighting again?"

"What does that have to do with anything?"

"Answer the question, Sophie."

"No, we're not. And most moms would ask if their kid is okay, especially with a crazy flu spreading throughout the lower forty-eight, and let them stay home from school if they're feeling sick." I glared up at her.

"Are we on the East Coast? Do you have a fever? How about any abdominal pain or vomiting?" She pursed her lips, awaiting my answer. When I said nothing, she lifted her brow triumphantly. "Sophie, you're always mopey when you guys fight," she said in rebuttal, and glanced at my phone cord, disappearing under my pillow. "And you sleep with your phone beside you, hoping he'll apologize first." She lifted an expectant eyebrow, then leaned down and rested the back of her hand against my forehead. Barely a breath passed before she shook her head. "No fever." Satisfied, she pinned her gaze on me. "Get up." She picked up my dirty clothes off the floor and tossed them into my hamper as she hurried back toward the door. "I'm serious," she warned. "And make sure you tell Katie you'll be out of school Friday."

I sat up, my head throbbing at the sudden movement. "What? Why am I missing school Friday?"

She spared me a glance—severe enough to be considered a glare—then disappeared down the hall. "Dr. Revis," she answered.

"Mom, I'm fine. I don't need to see the stupid bone doctor anymore. He said I was fine last time, I'll be fine this time."

"You just got done telling me you're sick!" she called, and her heels clacked against the kitchen tile floor as she rushed around.

"This is different, Mom. God—you're always so worried."

"Yes, I am." She poked her head in, knotting a scarf loosely around her neck. "I worry because you never do the hip and knee exercises you're supposed to in order to keep you strong. And don't even get me started on the insoles I paid a fortune for that you never wear."

"Mom—"

"You thought elementary school kids were mean? Well, Soph, teenagers are cruel. Don't forget how miserable you were in Florida before we left. Do you want to go back to feeling singled out, the way you used to?" I hated the way she dipped her chin, lifted an eyebrow, and stared at me skeptically all at the same time.

"Like the way you're making me feel right now?" I bit out. "Mom, no one is going to give me a hard time—"

"Get up, Sophie," she said with exasperation. "I won't say it again." She disappeared from the doorway and headed back down the hall.

"Fine, but I'm not going to see Dr. Revis!" I told her. "It's pointless." And I didn't need any more reminders of how different I was. I just wanted her to let me be a normal teenager for once.

Rolling my eyes, I flung my legs off the edge of the bed and studied my feet. I might've been slender and weak compared to some people, but I wasn't deformed—at least not anymore, even if it had taken a few rounds of special shoes and braces to make my bones grow that way. And while I wanted to appreciate my mom's concern, I wasn't sure she cared about how it affected me as much as how it affected her picture-perfect facade, even when the entire building knew it was all a sham—weak-ankled, club-footed daughter and all. What a shock she would get when she found out my weak bones were the least of my problems.

"I don't hear the shower!" she called.

"Gah!" I grabbed my phone and marched into the bathroom, slamming the door behind me. If she knew why I felt sick to my stomach, she'd forget all about Dr. Revis and stupid protein shakes.

My stomach rumbled and tears burned the backs of my eyes. It had been almost six weeks since I'd been with Jesse, and Google was plenty helpful when it came to ironing out the details about the rest.

My mom was so worried about what it would look like to have a broken daughter, she'd never forgive me for staining her reputation this way.

Shame swelled in my chest and fear tightened my throat as I turned the shower on.

My mom's knuckles rapped on the bathroom door, and I jumped, wiping the moisture from my eyes. "What?"

"Excuse you," she said coldly through the door. "I was just going to tell you to come home right after school. Your dad wants to video chat."

"Fine."

She muttered something inaudible as her heels clacked away, but all I could do was imagine my dad's already reserved expression pinching with shock and then hardening with rage as I told him that I'd done the one thing he made me promise never to do—

mirror the mistake that had plagued my parents' relationship since I was born.

Pulling my hair from my ponytail, I let the long, heavy strands fall around my shoulders, veiling me as I covered my face and cried.

TWO
ALEX

I traced a crooked square over and over with my pencil. Lead powder dusted the page of my spiral notebook, creased from being shoved in Jimmy's junk drawer since the beginning of time. Change was inevitable and something I was used to, even if it wasn't something I was all that comfortable with. Change meant uncertainty, and with it being my first day of school in a new town, today was anything but certain. I'd manage, though. I'd get by. I'd do what was needed.

My mind drifted as I waited for my new classmates to show. Whitely was as bizarre as a town could get—a once abandoned military base turned seaside harbor, overlooking the Prince William Sound. Save for the ships coming in and out of port through the Alaska Marine Highway, there were barely enough residents and tourists combined for Whitely to be considered a true city.

There was a single road leading in and out, manned by a single light that let cars enter and exit in rotation, and if that wasn't strange enough, the tunnel always closed after dark—or so I'd been warned. The monitored road might've served a purpose when the military was holed up here decades ago, but now it just felt claustrophobic; once you were in Whitely, you were stuck until the road opened again, forced to stay in a single building with the rest of the town with nowhere else to go. Unfortunately for me, I'd be trapped for another four months. I could only hope the courts dismissed my wardship from the foster care system once I turned eighteen.

I stared out at the snow-covered village, at the shipyard and tourist outposts. There wasn't much else to look at, except for the boats in the harbor. To me, Whitely was less like the touristy trading port it was known for, and more reminiscent of a Fallout nuclear-winter world. Especially when it seemed like half of the lower forty-eight was infected with the flu.

My gaze settled on the monstrous Heston Building less than a mile away, situated at the foot of the mountains that enclosed the town. The cracked and ruined military barracks were menacing to say the least, with broken, dark windows and a weather-ravaged stone face. It was built to be a stronghold, but instead was near collapse, and bred ghost stories known throughout Alaska. Offset and forgotten from the rest of the town, it was a building I wouldn't be exploring anytime soon. I half expected to see a putrid, flesh-eating zombie step into one of the dark voids and stare straight at me, warningly.

The barracks were the only other looming building in the cove, besides the apartment complex the school was attached to; the complex that would be my temporary home for the next 131 days, give or take. I'd gone from living in a dank, dark city one day, to a hidden hamlet the next. I wasn't sure which was worse, dangerous streets or claustrophobia.

"Staying with your uncle will keep you out of trouble until April." Digs might've thought he was right, but I wondered if that was possible. Not because I wanted to get into trouble, though sometimes making questionable decisions when hanging out with the wrong crowd seemed like the lesser of most evils. And it wasn't like I was always in trouble, but trouble definitely seemed

to find me everywhere I went—it always had, even as a little kid. For some reason, despite who and what my family was, I always had a hard time just walking away.

Once I saw the place my case manager was talking about though, I knew Digs was right. There was nothing to do in Whitely, short of skipping rocks and fishing. There was nowhere to go. There were no gangs or bad areas of town to worry about, at least not that I could see from where I sat. There weren't even neighborhoods.

The only threat to my good behavior and sanity here was my Uncle Jimmy himself. He was a first-rate asshole, yet somehow he'd convinced Digs some tough love would be good for me. Only, I wasn't sure Jimmy even knew how to spell *love*, even if he had *tough* down to a science with every scowl, grunt, and scratch of his junk. It was how Neanderthals expressed dominance, and it was obvious Jimmy hadn't evolved much in his forty-odd years.

My gaze shifted to the dark hallway. Bizarre as this place was, they had school on Mondays, right?

I glanced around the empty classroom, less than inspired. The windows were big, and dying plants in painted pots lined the sills. The room's stuffy, recirculated air made my nose tingle. Odd as it was, attached to the apartment complex for winter ease, I thought this might be the shittiest school I'd been to yet.

Much like the rest of the building, it felt more like a 1970s hotel—from the hum of the overhead lighting to the drab wall color and ribbed carpet floor—it was all leftovers from another era and needed major updates, the furnace especially.

I bunched my sweatshirt sleeves up to my elbows, and peered up at the ticking clock, hanging between two faded maps, one of Alaska and one of the United States. It was already a quarter to nine. Had Jimmy forgotten to tell me something? Was there a Monday morning roundup off-site? Had I read the painted numbers above the door outside incorrectly? Was this not the eleventh and twelfth grade classroom?

With a yawn, I leaned back in my chair. As much as I hated Jimmy's lumpy couch, at this rate, I could've caught a few more z's before schlepping down here, especially since the apartment had finally quieted down after Jimmy had left for work.

Yeah, Whitely was making it way too easy to skip school, and I was about to give up and find myself some breakfast, when I finally heard voices further down the hall.

Tapping my pencil on the chipped corner of the desk, I waited for my new classmates to come into view.

"—was great, Jeannie," a woman said, and my heartbeat kicked up a pace. Students trickled in through the door. White skin, tan skin, brown and red hair. A couple of the students were tall but most of them were short. There were a handful of them, and their mutterings faded as they paused just inside the doorway.

"Oh—" The woman I assumed was the teacher put her hand on one student's shoulder to steady herself as she practically careened into him. Then she smiled at me, her brown eyes crinkling. "You're the new student, Alejandro." Lifting her bag strap over her head, she walked over to her desk, her dirty-blonde ponytail swaying with each step.

"It's Alex, actually." I sat forward and continued tapping my pencil on the edge of the desk, studying the five new faces blinking at me. All of them but the teacher looked to be about my age, give or take a year or two.

The teacher set her bag on her desk chair. "Alex it is then," she chirped, and pointed to her head. "Mentally noted." She didn't look like any teacher I'd ever had before, young and smiling—she was even kinda hot. Definitely nothing like the comic book-loving string bean I had at East Anchorage High, or the macho chick at Bartlett who looked like she could kick my ass. I'm pretty sure she would've too, if it hadn't been considered child abuse. I was perpetually late to her class.

The carpet was old and bunched under the students' feet as they weaved through the desks to their seats. The shock of seeing a new face had worn off, and they bickered and chatted like they'd known each other for years, only flicking cursory glances in my direction.

Remotely, I wondered why there were seats enough for fifteen students if there were only a handful of us. It was getting closer to Christmas, so they were probably all faraway somewhere, traveling or whatever happy families did during the holidays.

"So, am I early or something?" I watched as they all casually took their seats. There were no late bells and there was clearly zero urgency to sit down, though it was almost nine.

"Excuse me?" The teacher glanced up from her notebook. I nodded to the clock above the door. "Oh—no, not really. Things were a little chaotic this morning. I was gone last week due to a family illness out of town. So, Tyler and Jeannie were showing me how their science project was coming along in the greenhouse up on the top floor."

A girl with freckles and red hair looked intriguingly over at me. Tyler, I assumed, nudged her with his elbow to get out of his way as he plopped into the desk beside her.

"At any rate, welcome to class." The teacher gestured around the room. "Sorry we weren't here to greet you properly." She was what I would've expected an elementary school teacher to be like, animated and sweet. She didn't look old enough to be a high school teacher, at least not with a name like Mrs. Gunner, or was it Mrs. Anderson? I'd imagined a salt and pepper haired older woman with glasses and a kind smile, for some reason.

"I'm Mrs. Gunderson, but everyone calls me Katie," she said, pulling out a folder from her bag.

I wasn't sure I could handle all the *strange* in this place and also call my teacher by her first name, so I mentally opted to call her Mrs. Gunderson.

"The rules are fairly loose here, as long as your work gets done," she continued, and flipped through the file in her hand. Her eyebrows pinched together within seconds, then she glanced at me again, her expression narrowing slightly.

It was a file about me, obviously.

"This is a much smaller school than you're used to," she said with a nervous laugh. "Isn't it?" It wasn't a real question, because that was evident. It was a smaller school than just about anyone outside of Whitely had ever been to. "We might be less structured than what you're accustomed to, Alex, but we expect students to behave with respect and get their work done on time. There are consequences for misconduct, but hopefully we won't have to get into any of that. Think of us more like a family—*your* family." Her smile broadened again. "That being said, welcome to Whitely."

She must've read the part about juvie and the bullshit assault and battery accusations from last year. They dropped the charges, but it was still a stain on my name, one of many, and I was glad they could be expunged on my eighteenth birthday, like they were never there at all.

"There's a lot to get up to speed on, including choosing a science project that we're well into already. We'll figure something out though," she said pleasantly. "Have you received a tour of the building yet? We aren't always learning out of the classroom or working out in the gymnasium."

I shook my head.

"We'll see if Tyler or someone can show you around before school tomorrow. There's a movie room on the twelfth floor, and city council meetings are on the thirteenth floor on the first Tuesday of every month, which I offer extra credit to attend."

I shrugged. "I have free time. I can explore the building on my own." It would take all of an hour, I thought wryly.

"Oh, great." Mrs. Gunderson inhaled, and gripped the back of her swivel chair. The cushion indented as her fingers pressed into it more tightly, like she was steadying herself for whatever came next. "So, Alex, why don't you tell us about yourself?" She gestured to the other students, all of them looking at me.

I wasn't sure if it was the recycled air pumping through the building, or if all the gawking faces were getting to me, but heat swirled over my skin, and I pushed my long sleeves creeping down my arm back up to my elbows. "Uh—I'm Alex," I said. "I just moved here from Anchorage—"

The door creaked opened and a strawberry blonde peeked inside. "Sorry I'm late," she said, her face flushed as she glanced at the teacher.

"Oh, good—Sophie, you came."

Sophie took a seat two rows over, oblivious to me, unlike the rest of them. But she was harder to miss. Sophie was tall and slender, with long hair that brushed the middle of her back. She was pretty, in a preppy, ripped jeans, and off-the-shoulder sweater kinda way, with her fancy Ugg boots. Normally I would write her off as a rich girl—prom queen material for sure—only she was quiet and meek as she settled into her desk, unlike Jeannie who kept looking at me with hungry appreciation.

"I heard Jesse was home sick," Mrs. Gunderson said. I wasn't sure if Jesse was Sophie's brother or sister, but Mrs. Gunderson's expression turned sullen. "I'm glad you're feeling okay. With all the commotion in the lower forty-eight, even the littlest flu is frightening."

Sophie frowned. "I didn't know—" She paused when her blue eyes met mine. She straightened in her seat, looked up at Mrs. Gunderson again, then continued. "I haven't talked to him since Friday, so I didn't know he was sick."

"He better not come back if he's sick," Jeannie said, twirling a red strand of hair around her finger. "I *can't* get sick."

"Why not," Tyler muttered, "because it's bad for your complexion?" He laughed, but no one else did.

"Not in here, Tyler. You know the rules." Mrs. Gunderson was capable of a somewhat commanding tone, which was surprising.

"That's her brother," the guy next to me whispered. "They fight all the time. She's one year younger."

I nodded as Jeannie looked at me for the third time. I'd seen the same look that was on her face a dozen times between four different schools—I was the new kid with a less than shining reputation, and girls were attracted to it like a leprechaun to a pot of gold. It was like my rap sheet was plastered to my forehead everywhere I went. Girls like Jeannie could sniff me out, latch on long enough to feel a sense of danger, then they'd get bored and move on when they realized I wasn't as dangerous as they'd imagined. Not only was I uninterested in Jeannie, I was planning on staying miles away from her.

"Sophie," Mrs. Gunderson continued, "this is Alex. He's new to Whitely, obviously. He was just about to tell us a bit about himself. But for those of you who haven't already heard, Alex is Jimmy's nephew."

"Jimmy Hart has a nephew?" Jeannie spat, blinking at me like she was beyond confused. "Isn't Jimmy too young to have a nephew?"

"*Ortiz*, idiot. Not Hart." Tyler scoffed. "Can't you see the resemblance?"

My knuckles whitened as I gripped the edge of the desk. Although Tyler likely referred to my exotic bronze skin color and nothing more, Jimmy was the last person on the entire planet I ever wanted to be compared to. He was a deadbeat loser who was past his prime and plummeting quickly to a washed-up has-been. The entire building would have to be blind not to notice.

Mrs. Gunderson cleared her throat. "As I was saying, this is Alex *Ortiz*," she emphasized as she outstretched her hand to me, like a portrait on display. I stole a quick glance at the small lotus tattoo on her wrist, surprisingly pleased Mrs. Gunderson had a bit of a wild side too, it seemed.

All the students stared at me expectantly, except for Sophie. She was preoccupied with her phone.

"Soph," Mrs. Gunderson hedged.

Startled, Sophie pushed her phone to the corner of her desk, blinking at the teacher before she turned to look at me, or more like she was looking *through* me. Her blue eyes gleamed with sadness.

Mrs. Gunderson nodded. "Go ahead, Alex."

I cleared my throat. "Like I said, I'm Alex. I'm staying here until April."

"Why?" Jeannie asked. "What happens in April?"

"On the tenth, I turn eighteen and I can leave," I told her. I could taste the freedom merely thinking about it.

"Where were you before?" She blinked at me with sincere interest. "No one comes here because they want to," she muttered the last part with a smile.

Even though I didn't want to tell stories about my life, like we were sitting around the campfire in need of entertainment, I had to tell them something or they would keep staring. "I was living with a foster family in Anchorage. It didn't work out," I said plainly. "Now I'm here."

I was grateful when Mrs. Gunderson cleared her throat. "Are you looking into any colleges, Alex? I've been helping Tyler, Jesse, and Sophie with their applications. Maybe I could help you with yours too."

I glanced at Sophie, her foot bouncing as she bit her middle fingernail, staring at the blank screen of her phone. "Yeah, maybe," I said so Mrs. Gunderson would move on, but the answer was no. I wouldn't be in Whitely long enough to worry about school. I'd worry about my GED later, after I got out of here and could live my life for myself instead of for adults who cared more about a monthly check than anything having to do with me. It wasn't like I could afford to go to college anyway.

"Well, we can circle back to that after class. We better get started." Mrs. Gunderson clapped her hands together.

I heaved out an exhausted breath, glad my pointless introduction was over, and glanced over at Sophie still staring down at her phone.

"Jeannie, can you pass these out for me, please?" She handed a small stack of papers to Jeannie in the front row. "As I mentioned before I left," Mrs. Gunderson continued, addressing everyone. "We're talking about the Revolutionary War this week. And we may or may not have a pop quiz on who the key players were and how it ended." She laughed at her none too subtle warning as she scribbled on the whiteboard.

"Here you go." Jeannie appeared beside my desk. Her red hair was up in a half ponytail, her eyes thick with black makeup, and her clothes tight enough to appreciate her feminine curves. She grinned fully this time—not just a smirk, and a dimple formed in her cheek, which I wasn't expecting.

"Thanks." I smiled back, and took the handout. Leaning back in my chair, I admired the sway of her hips as she weaved her way through the rows, handing out two more papers before glancing back at me.

"Alex," Mrs. Gunderson warned with a lifted eyebrow. I'd already been caught flirting, but in all fairness it was Jeannie, not me. Mrs. Gunderson grabbed a textbook off the shelf beneath the window and walked it over to me. "Page forty-seven. You're getting a crash course in the Siege of Yorktown."

I didn't get further than writing my name at the top of the page, when my gaze traveled to Sophie again as she tapped her pen on the side of her book. Apparently I wasn't the only anxious one today, and by the looks of it, I'd say she was on the brink of tears.

THREE
SOPHIE

The first couple hours of class felt more like eons. Class was the last place I wanted to be right now. That is, until the new guy came to sit beside me for our chapter review exercises.

I glanced at him from the corner of my eye. As far as a summary partner went, he caught on more quickly than I'd expected. He remembered the answer to every question without writing them down. Meanwhile, I could barely focus on what we were supposed to be studying to begin with.

"I don't know how, I just remember random shit sometimes," he explained. Even though Alex was the new kid, somehow I was the one who felt out of place.

"All right," Katie said from the front of the room. "Time to wrap it up for a bit. I can hear your stomachs growling from here."

"Finally," Alex grumbled, and slammed his book shut. The rest of the classroom did the same and moved back to their seats, but I couldn't help but watch Alex as he gathered a ratty notebook covered in Sharpie doodles. Then he picked up his broken pencil. *Intriguing*, that was a word for him.

"Thanks," I said. "For the study help, I mean."

He looked over his shoulder, then nodded, if a bit reluctantly. He was nice enough—and cute even, in a bad boy sort of way—but none of that mattered, not when my life was essentially over.

I wrapped my hands around my stomach and slouched back into my seat. It wasn't hunger that had my tummy rumbling, but pure dread and fear. I *hated* fear—it made me feel weaker than I already was.

Letting my head fall back, I squeezed my eyes shut and took a calming, deep breath as Katie explained the essay prompt for after lunch.

A child is not the end of the world. I had to keep telling myself that or risk a breakdown in front of everyone. Women did it every day around the world and in worse circumstances than mine, and with worse partners, even if Jesse was the type of guy who would rather lie to avoid conflict than admit the condom broke the last time we had sex and own up to it.

"Enjoy your lunch break!" Katie called, as a patter of footsteps hurried out of the classroom. "Are you all right, Sophie?"

"What?" My eyes flew open, and Katie stood from her desk. Cheeks beet red, I smiled. "Yes. Sorry. I'm just worried about Jesse, that's all." I cleared my throat and tucked my hair behind my ear as I gathered my things. "I didn't sleep well either, with all the talk about the outbreak on the East Coast—"

"Oh, that's right. Bailey's there, visiting her grandma." Katie tilted her head with understanding. "I can see why you'd be so worried. I'm sure she's fine. Her parents will keep her safe."

I forced another smile as I clipped my bag closed. "Yeah, I'm sure you're right."

Katie smiled encouragingly and rubbed my shoulder. "Maybe you can give her a call during lunch and see how she's doing. She could probably use a friend." Katie headed back toward the front of the class.

I tried to steady a deep inhale as I praised myself on the quickest save ever. If Katie looked too closely, she'd know I was lying. That's what happened when your teacher was your neighbor, your friends were your building mates, and *everyone* knew your parents.

My half-ass plan to buy a pregnancy test at lunch would not go unnoticed either. I scanned the hallway and first-floor layout in my memory, mapping out the building to estimate how long it would take me to get from the store to the restroom, then maybe to Jesse's to tell him off, and back again—all before lunch break ended. Jesse might've been sick with a cold, but he wasn't dying. He could at least text me back.

But who was I kidding? There was no way I could buy a test without anyone knowing, not unless I was going to steal it, and getting *caught* . . . That was an entirely new problem I hadn't considered.

I combed my fingers through my hair. The tension in my shoulders was so tight, I was surprised I could move my neck. Pulling my bag over my shoulder, I glanced at Katie. "I'm going to grab lunch and call Bailey. I'll be back in thirty or so."

Katie waved me away, mid-gulp from her thermos, and I headed out the door without looking back. The clomp of my Ugg boots echoed in the hallway between school and the apartment complex.

The air in the hallway was suddenly too warm and thick as I walked toward the main floor. I fanned my face, praying it was a wave of anxiety and not a heat flash or some other unwanted symptom.

Or maybe the blaze of hell is inching closer to me with each step. That's where my mom would condemn me, and not because she was religious, just *really* strict and severe when she wanted to be. I had to swallow down the impending wave of nausea that bubbled up with every step.

Would she make me get rid of the baby? The thought suddenly dawned on me. Did I *want* to get rid of it? I was in the exact situation my mom told me never to get myself into. It was one of two things she'd always lectured me about—my posture and pregnancy at the age of eighteen. This wasn't something she could lecture away with a severely disappointed finger wag though. In fact, she would probably kill me when she found out, and she of all people could get away with it too. As the mayor, she knew the coroner and was close with the doctor. She had the police in her pocket, and she could bury my body out in the snow. No one would be any the wiser.

But hysterical thoughts aside, another scandal after my dad's infidelity would ruin her, and it wasn't her career I was concerned about. Mentally and emotionally, she would be wrecked.

Biting my lip, I followed the signs to the mercantile area, though I didn't need them to know where I was going. I was going to have to buy a pregnancy test from the market, and I prayed for Carlyle or Henry to be behind the counter when I got there; they'd be so incredibly awkward they would pretend they didn't see the pink and white box entirely—unlike Evelyn or Jonesy.

Murmurs met my ears as I came to the split in the hallway; straight ahead for the managerial offices, the market, and video store; left for the indoor pool with cracked tiling and the fitness room with dangerously old equipment.

I continued straight; toward Mr. Han, one of the yacht captains; my classmate Sarah Michaels, who I'd only just realized wasn't in class today; her mom; and *crap*. Henry. I needed him to be working at the market, and there he was standing alongside the others—each of them with masks over their faces—outside Dr. Harwick's clinic. It was a clinic large enough for only one hospital bed and an examination table, and given the number of residents in the building, a waiting area hadn't really been necessary, until now, at least.

A shiver ran down my spine when I saw the red in Sarah's eyes. Suddenly, I grew more worried about Bailey, and then for Jesse. The news covered the flu outbreak, and we knew it was really bad in some areas, but this was Alaska, there was nothing here. There were cities and towns, but they were few and far between, and hundreds—in some cases thousands—of miles of snow stretched out in between.

But I knew better than that. Viruses didn't care about the cold. They thrived in live, warm bodies, and there were plenty of them coming in and out of Alaska every day.

"Are you okay, Sarah?" I asked, nearly breathless.

Sarah's eyes met mine with a slow blink. "I—"

"She just needs the flu shot," her mother said quickly. "She gets sick every year. This is nothing new." Though Mrs. Michaels' voice was flippant, I hadn't seen Sarah sick before, at least not like this. She was in her wrinkled pajamas, and her skin was almost green. Her wavy brown hair was nappy around her face, and her eyes—I couldn't stop staring at them.

"Carol," Dr. Harwick called from inside the clinic, and Mrs. Michaels tugged on Sarah's hand as she strode inside. I wasn't sure if Jesse was that sick, but if he felt as bad as Sarah looked, I almost felt bad for being annoyed with him.

Then my stomach churned and I remembered the severity of the problem at hand. I could only *pray* I was sick at this point. But even though I felt like crap, it wasn't like any flu I'd ever had before. I could feel something inside of me changing. Was that what a mother's intuition felt like? Was pregnancy something I could feel in my bones—a warmth just beneath the surface of my skin, pushing the blood through my veins with more ferocity than anything I'd ever felt before, like it was preparing for something?

Grabbing my phone from my pocket, I decided to call Bailey and continued down the hallway toward the market. I passed the elevators and hurried by the managerial offices, specifically my mom's door—grateful it was closed, then I dialed my best friend. I needed to make sure she was okay.

"Please pick up. Please pick up . . ." But I had no idea what time it was in Connecticut or if she was at the hospital with her grandma. When she didn't answer, I whimpered and shoved my phone into the back pocket of my jeans.

Swallowing thickly, I stopped outside the market, just shy of the window. Since Henry was at the clinic, Carlyle was my only saving grace, and I willed him to be behind the checkout counter. But when I leaned forward, I was instantly more depressed.

Evelyn was working the counter, eyes wide and worried as she talked to my *mom* at the register. Sucking in a breath, I turned to run back down the hall before my mom could see me and collided with a warm, firm body that smelled shower-fresh.

"Shit," I hissed, stumbling backward.

Alex reached out to grab my arm and steady me. "You okay?"

"Fine," I spat, and tucked my hair behind my ears. "What are you doing here?"

"Getting lunch," he said wryly. "What about you? Did you change your mind?"

I glowered at him. "What are you talking about?"

"You were about to go in." He nodded to the store.

Crap. "Yes." And my mom was still inside. I hurried down an offshoot of the hallway, toward the maintenance room and the public bathrooms.

"Hey—are you okay?" Alex's footsteps were heavy and right behind me.

"Yes, just—leave me alone, okay?" I wasn't sure exactly where my legs were taking me, just that it needed to be somewhere my mom couldn't see the guilt on my face. I could never lie to her. She would know the moment I did, and I wasn't ready to talk to her about it.

Alex followed me to the maintenance closet and stopped outside the open door.

"What are you doing?" I bit out, prepared to pull the door shut.

"What are *you* doing?" He stood in the doorway for everyone to see.

I glanced down the hall, worried my mom would see, and pulled him inside, closing the door behind him.

Turning around, I stumbled into a mop bucket, sending it clanging onto its side. The closet was small and the space between Alex and I was . . . tight, which I hadn't thought through.

I flicked on the light.

Alex's smile spread the width of his face, and I hated to admit I liked it—especially seeing he was clearly entertained by all of this. "Do you always hide in the broom closet?"

"Of course not."

He took a deep breath, his dark features more like ebony in the sharp shadows cast by the swinging light.

"Why did you follow me? Now you've made it weird," I told him, and turned to crack the door open.

"*I'm* making it weird? You just pulled me into a dark room and locked us inside."

I didn't justify his question with an answer as I peered down the hall, watching my mom cross the corridor. She had her cellphone to her ear and about a dozen water bottles in her arms, which I thought was strange, then she disappeared from view. I didn't care what she was doing, as long as she was gone.

As my heart slid from my throat down into my chest, and settled back into a less frenzied pace, I stepped out into the hallway.

Alex walked out behind me.

I glanced at him, though he said nothing. He didn't have to. I knew he was waiting for an explanation, but I hurried back down the hallway. I could feel his expectant stare boring into the back of my skull as his footsteps followed.

I whipped around. "What, Alex?"

His eyebrow rose, and he tilted his head with a shrug. "I'm going to the market," he drawled. "To get food, for lunch . . ." He said it like he had to remind me, like I didn't know the minutes were counting down.

I needed to figure out what the hell I was going to do before I ran out of time. "Yeah, me too," I said quickly. With a huff, I turned on my heel, too distressed about my predicament to worry about him. But the instant I got to the market, I froze in the doorway. I still didn't have a plan.

Alex stepped inside, the chime dinging, and Evelyn looked up from her crossword, eyeing him closely. She liked gossip, which meant she was more intrigued than most to see a new face.

I took a step backward out of Evelyn's view. She was one of my mom's close friends. There was no way I could do this with her here. I would wait; I had no other choice. I would make Jesse take me to the store when he was feeling better, or I would wait for Henry's shift—whenever that was. I didn't have to know at this very moment, it wouldn't change anything.

My heartbeat thudded harder, my chest heaving up and down as I glanced from the doorway to the pregnancy tests I could see in the far aisle from where I stood. It was so close; I could walk in and take one and hope for the best, if I only had the courage to do it.

"Are you on meds or something?"

"What?" My eyes darted to Alex as he stepped out of the store; a paper bag and a Pepsi in his hand.

"Or do you need money?" He lifted an incredulous shoulder. "You know, to buy the lunch you said you were getting." His eyes narrowed on me, like I was crazy—I *was* crazy, for today at least. "But you were lying about that, weren't you," he realized.

I swallowed. "Yes, I was lying. What's it matter to you?"

Alex shrugged again and made a move to walk past me.

"Wait, Alex—" I licked my lips, unable to look him in the eye and feeling sicker by the minute. "Sorry. I'm having a really, *really* bad day. Now's not exactly a good time to get to know each other." I gripped my bag strap tighter.

"What do you mean, *this isn't the time*?" he said, and when I looked at him, his mouth curved into a smile. "We just spent half of our lunchbreak in the broom closet together. I'd say we know each other well enough." His eyebrows danced, and my chest rose with a quick laugh.

I couldn't help but smile in return. I appreciated the joke, even if it was ridiculous.

Satisfied, Alex nodded and continued past me. He had an easy stride about him, which I found almost as fascinating as his smile. How was it he was so calm and confident? I envied him in that moment and my smile quickly faded.

My gaze landed on a stack of off-brand pregnancy tests directly beside a few boxes of Trojan condoms, at the end of the farthest of the store's five aisles. *Oh, the irony.*

I did a double take as Alex stepped up beside me. His brow crinkled with concern. "Are you okay? Seriously." He didn't hedge and his voice didn't waver. It was thick and low with concern.

I tried to smile for both of our sakes, but I couldn't force it. My mom had brushed off my being sick like I was making the whole thing up, and while I might've stretched the truth a little, I was definitely not fine, and she didn't even care. Yet Alex, a complete stranger a few hours ago, was looking at me like he actually, truly cared what my answer would be, and I nearly lost it.

"No," I admitted. "Not really. I'm freaking out." I inhaled a deep breath, trying to hold it together a little longer. Then I exhaled and cleared my throat. "But I'll survive." I glanced into the store a final time.

"Oh," he said, staring in the same direction. "I see . . ."

A swirl of heat traveled through my chest and up my neck to my cheeks. I was somewhere between cherry and sunburn red; I could feel shame emanating through the skin on my face. "Yeah, like I said, you can't help me."

"You don't want the cashier to know?"

"Ha. No. Evelyn is one of *the* chattiest old women in this place. I might as well put a scarlet P on my stomach now so that everyone knows."

Alex handed me his Pepsi and the paper bag in his hand. "Take this."

I did so automatically, then he turned for the store. "Wait—Alex—" I reached for his arm, but it was too late. He walked back into the market without hesitation, beelining for the pharmacy aisle.

FOUR
SOPHIE

Frantic, I glanced around to make sure no one was watching and retreated a few more steps back into the corridor that led to the broom closet.

Evelyn hadn't seen me. She won't know it's for me. There was no way she could.

I pulled out my phone to make it look as though I was waiting for someone without a care in the world. But inside, my heart was a battering ram, and I thought I might hyperventilate if Alex didn't return soon.

I waited like that, scrolling through Facebook posts on my phone, not registering any of them as the minutes ticked by. My face grew hotter and my heart raced in my ears more loudly with every passing minute. It felt like an eternity before Alex finally appeared in the mouth of the hallway. He continued past me, toward the elevator, with another brown paper bag in his hand.

I glanced at the market to make sure no one was watching and walked as casually as I could behind him, peering down at the blank screen on my phone shaking in my hands. When we were both inside the elevator, just the two of us, he hit the button for the eighth floor. The instant the door closed, he handed me the bag and took his lunch and Pepsi back.

"I can't believe you did that," I hissed, adrenaline zipping through me. My heart had never raced so fast—never felt like it was going to pop out of my chest like aliens did in the movies.

"You're welcome," he grumbled, and took a long pull from his soda bottle. It was like it was whiskey to a drunk. He was nervous too—or maybe embarrassed.

"You really didn't have to do that," I said, still shocked that he had, and his unexpected kindness brought the threat of more tears to my eyes.

"I didn't? You were hyperventilating in the hallway, so I think I did. Besides," he said with a shrug, and I wondered if he wasn't as calm as his exterior let on, "everyone already knows I'm a screwup, they probably think I already got a girl pregnant."

I snorted. "You've barely been here a few days, that seems like a stretch."

Alex shrugged. "Trust me, no one will be surprised if Mrs. Chatterbox decides to say something."

"But," I shook my head, "You don't even know me."

"Yeah, well, I did it anyway. Now *you're* just making it weird," he said, staring at the door. I eyed him in the metal reflection, while he watched the numbers on the screen ticking higher. His thoughtful silence was strangely unwanted.

"I'm not a slut," I blurted, feeling the need to explain. "Jesse and I—he's been my boyfriend for almost a year. I just—we screwed up."

"You *don't* have to explain yourself to me," he said holding up his palm.

But I felt like I did. "It's just—"

"*Seriously.*" It was more of a plea than a courtesy. "I really don't want to know."

I nodded, dazed as I licked my lips, and turned to face my reflection in the elevator door again. I knew nothing about Alex other than he was taller than me, maybe even six-feet tall, with broad shoulders and a charismatic smile. More than anything, I knew that Alex was compassionate, even if he was a troublemaker or whatever he'd been labeled in his life before he came to Whitely. And I'd never appreciated a stranger more.

"I just hope he's not a douchebag," he said in a low voice. "For your sake."

I blinked at him.

The doors dinged open as we arrived on the eighth floor, and Alex stepped out without another word or look in my direction.

"Where are you going?" I asked. I glanced down the hall toward Jesse's apartment.

He held up his lunch bag. "I've gotta heat my burrito up somehow."

I'd forgotten all about Jimmy and that he lived on the same floor.

Without thought, I stepped out of the elevator and reached for Alex's arm as he turned to leave. My grip was more desperate than I'd meant, and the moment he turned around, staring at my hand on his bicep, I took a spacious step back, though I could still see the luminescent golden honey in Alex's eyes from the overhead lights.

He tilted his head, waiting for me to get on with it.

"Thank you," I told him. The paper bag crackled in my tightening grip. I searched for something else to say that wasn't so dumb, but the same words rolled off my tongue. "Just—thank you."

Alex glanced from my stomach to my face, making me blush. He wasn't checking me out, I reminded myself. He was taking my craziness in, or perhaps my sincerity. *He was reminding himself that I was likely pregnant, and a complete and utter mess.*

"You're welcome." His voice was softer than I expected, and in that moment, Alex was calm water in a dark storm, and his kindness sent a tear over the brim of my lashes.

"I owe you one," I whispered, offering him a small smile.

He didn't nod or shake his head. Instead, he continued down the hall to his uncle's apartment. "Good luck, Sophie," he muttered.

"Thank you," I whispered again, though I didn't think he could hear me. His broad shoulders seemed to slump the closer he drew to the apartment, his stride less confident. With a deep breath, he opened the front door and disappeared inside, the door latching behind him.

FIVE
ALEX

Before the door even closed, Jimmy was glaring at me. Amidst the scent of stale beer wafting from the empty beer cans in the kitchen and on the side table in the living room, there was a hint of freshness in the apartment, like Jimmy had just gotten out of the shower, again.

"Aren't you supposed to be in school?"

Jimmy had been sober when I'd first arrived, and as the days went on and he drank more and more, his mismatched but tidy apartment turned into a garbage pit. I couldn't help but wonder if he thought showering hid his drunkenness.

I lifted my burrito. "Lunch break." I walked around his recliner and couch, and into the galley kitchen. Judge Judy blared from the TV on the entertainment stand. It was janky, both the TV and the stand, but I didn't expect much from Jimmy. Everything he had looked like it had been salvaged from the community dumpster.

"You didn't bring me a burrito?"

I rolled my eyes. "I figured you'd still be at work."

Jimmy groused from his recliner and lay further back, making the springs squeak. "I decided to work a half day."

"I didn't realize you could choose your own hours."

He shrugged. "There's been an issue with the stupid heater for months. Can you believe they had some guys I've never even seen down there working on it over the weekend, like I can't do my job or something?"

I couldn't help it, my eyebrows lifted of their own accord. I feared he was asking me the question seriously, and I had to refrain from answering it.

"If they keep getting me the wrong parts, then of course it ain't gonna get fixed—simple as that. I swear someone tampered with the gas manifold. It's like they're trying to get me fired." Jimmy tossed the rest of his beer back and sighed. "Now they're gonna undermine me and bring in some fancy engineers from the city? I'll show them," he muttered.

Why did the Ortiz family seem to think anyone from the city was considered *fancy*? I'd lived in a lot of city neighborhoods, and none of them were fancy. My mother's words to me the day I'd told her I wanted to go to college had stuck with me since she said them.

"You think you're better than this life—that some fancy college will take you? Who's going to pay for that, your abuela? That woman turned her back on me when I needed her, she'll do the same thing to you."

Jimmy came from the same gene pool as my mother, so I guess I shouldn't have been surprised, though the memory of both her and my grandma sat too close to the surface for comfort. I'd gotten used to pushing away the darker memories, but being around Jimmy made it more difficult. His eyes were like my mother's, dark and deadened in a way that had been seared in my mind since the day she died. While she might've been a meth-head, he was clearly a drunk. I knew there was a difference, but it was hard to see past that when Jimmy's first question to me after Digs had left me in Jimmy's care was when he could expect his first check.

"I need a nap," he said with a stretch.

"Must be nice," I muttered, unwrapping my burrito.

"What was that?" he growled.

Cereal bowls were crusted with old milk and dried flakes. Beer cans were overflowing from the garbage bin. Of course none of that had been there when Digs dropped me off Friday to see my temporary home.

"Nothing," I muttered.

"Give me half of that," he said, his eyes glued to the TV.

"Dude, this is my lunch. I'm hungry. Have another bowl of cereal or something."

Jimmy sneered. "Digs told me you were ungrateful."

"No, I'm broke, there's a difference."

"Not too broke to buy a Pepsi with it," he countered.

"If you had more food in the house, I wouldn't have to spend my last five dollars on said burrito and Pepsi." I might've had a few more bucks than that, but Jimmy didn't need to know.

"Oh, so you're a smartass," he grumbled. "Fantastic."

I wanted to growl back at him, but I let it go. What the hell was I going to say? *Yeah, and you're a douche, so we're even.* The least he could do was make sure there was food. I had exactly twenty-eight dollars left to my name after buying that pregnancy test, which I hadn't expected to do, or for it to be so expensive. But then, I'd never bought a pregnancy test before.

I pulled my burrito out of the microwave and sat at the counter, wondering if Sophie was at her place, taking the test right now.

While I didn't think I should care if she was pregnant or not, I still couldn't help but wonder. She was a stranger, for the most part, but I saw the horror in her eyes, the fear. Even if I'd never had to worry about being pregnant before, I'd had plenty of other scares in my life—fights that could've ended much worse than they had, near misses and arrests, a broken heart when I was sixteen, or so I thought at the time—and I knew better than anyone that it wasn't easy steering clear from bad decisions all the time, and hindsight was a complete bitch.

Plus, my grandma would roll over in her grave if I hadn't helped Sophie.

I took a warm bite of beans, cheese, and flour tortilla as Jimmy's cell phone rang.

"This is Jimmy," he said with a yawn. "You mean those yahoos from Anchorage didn't fix the furnace over the weekend? What do you mean?" He paused to listen, and I continued to inhale my lunch. I only had ten minutes until I needed to be back in class.

"I'm talking about the guys I saw in there yesterday." Jimmy threw his arm up. "I'm not lying, Mayor," he ground out. "Fine, but I can't look at it until tomorrow. I've got too many house calls today. Threaten me all you want, Tessa, but I'm all you got. Tomorrow. Yeah, fine."

Jimmy dropped his cell into his lap and sighed as he lay further back in his chair. "Grab me a beer, would you?" he said over his shoulder.

I glared at his lazy ass in the recliner, wondering how a guy who showered twice a day could still be so gross. His hair was greased back, his clothes too big. People had to know he was a lazy piece of shit, right? Clearly he had this job because the building manager—and even the mayor—had no other option. Even I could do a better job than him, and I knew nothing about HVAC and boiler rooms.

I stared at the balled up paper bag on the counter and took another bite of burrito. I needed a job while I was here. Something to get me out of the house and put some money in my pocket, because clearly I was going to need it. And while Whitely didn't seem like the sort of place with a list of employment opportunities for teenagers, Sophie might know where I could find work. She did say she owed me a favor.

Jimmy's recliner creaked. "That beer?" he prompted, nodding to the fridge. "Grab one, would ya?"

With a swallow, I stood up and grabbed Jimmy a can from the fridge. I refrained from tossing it at him and walked it over. He didn't bother looking up from Judge Judy. "Stupid fuck," he grumbled at the plaintiff, then he laughed.

Yeah, stupid fuck indeed.

SIX
SOPHIE

Negative.

I sat on the vanity countertop in the bathroom, staring at the second pregnancy test. Fear. Cowardice. Whichever it was, I couldn't bring myself to take the test during lunch, knowing I'd have to go back to class and likely have to pretend everything was okay, when it was far from it. So I waited until I got home from school, and for what? Had all the fear and hesitation really been for nothing?

Dark had long since crept in through the bathroom window, and I flicked the main light on to be certain the shadows weren't playing tricks on me. The second test read the same as the first one, and I hesitated to breathe. Was it fortuitous that Alex had gotten a two-pack of tests, or had he done that on purpose? More importantly, had I done something wrong, twice? The directions seemed simple enough. Yet, as the single blue line brightened on the indicator, I nearly cried with relief.

False alarm. I was not pregnant.

My life was not over—my mom would *never* have to know.

I waited for all of the coiled tension in my neck and shoulders to ease, for the churning contents of my stomach to settle, but aside from the prick of happy, grateful tears in my eyes, there was no physical relief. In fact, my stomach lurched, and I slid off the vanity and onto the bathroom floor, heaving up the crackers I'd forced myself to eat when I'd returned home.

My stomach twisted and I heaved again. After what remained of the crackers was out and my mouth was watering with nothing else to give, the wave of nausea passed. It would take time, I realized, for the anxiety to go away.

Climbing to my feet, I turned on the sink and slurped water from my hand, rinsing the bile from my mouth. I put toothpaste on my toothbrush and brushed my teeth, thoughts consumed momentarily by Alex. Part of me felt guilty for not thinking about Jesse instead, but I couldn't help it.

Alex had surprised me. He'd said himself that helping me would add to whatever rap sheet he already had, and he'd done it anyway. And for who, a girl he probably looked at as the mayor's spoiled daughter? I hoped that wasn't what he thought. Especially since I'd already acted crazy, and he *definitely* thought I was rude. After everything he'd done, I hadn't even offered to pay him back —something I hadn't realized until I got back to school to find out Katie cancelled class due to her kids being sick. Alex had bolted before I could even pull out my wallet.

Tomorrow. I would pay him back tomorrow.

I hoped my mom would be on her Skype call with my dad, so that I could disappear into my bedroom for the night without rehashing my attitude from this morning. She'd already sent me on errands all afternoon, calling me with a list of things she needed me to get ready for an impromptu city council meeting. *"Consider it your apology."*

I stared at my reflection, comparing myself to Jeannie. Alex had been staring at her a lot. She'd made it easy for him with her dark fanning eyelashes and full-lip grin.

I rolled my eyes. It's not like it mattered. I needed to think about Jesse. He still hadn't returned my calls or texts. I was beginning to worry about him. I considered heading down to the eighth floor to see him and get rid of the pregnancy tests on my way down in the process.

I took the roll of toilet paper off the holder and grabbed the first test from the garbage. I wrapped it in paper until it was completely covered and looked like a fluffy white ball. I did the same with the other test. I wasn't going to walk around the apartment with them, so I stashed them in an empty Q-tips box discarded in the trash, along with a toilet paper roll and some balled up tissue, and shoved the box in the trash for safe keeping.

As the nausea settled a bit more, and I could breathe without a writhing, clawing feeling inside my chest, I flicked the light switch off before I stepped out into the hallway.

The living room was quiet and lit only by the soft glow of the Christmas lights around the bay window and the overhead light above the stove, which hadn't been cooked on in days. If it weren't for my room, you'd never know people actually lived here.

The sapphire-colored throw pillows were perfectly fluffed and staggered across the tan, suede couch, positioned in the middle of the room. The TV remote was nowhere to be seen, which meant it was in its assigned drawer, and besides the honeysuckle candle placed perfectly in the center, there were no other signs of life or disarray on the coffee table. Earthenware coasters weren't strewn around with dusty water glasses, like they would have been in my room, but stacked beneath my mom's favorite Tiffany Falling Leaves lamp on the side table. Everything was always as it should be, my mom made certain of it.

Her desk, centered against the wall behind the couch, however, grabbed my attention. My dad's mail stack was becoming more of a tower, and I wondered how much longer he'd be gone for work. Another three weeks? More? For my mom's sake, I hoped it was less.

Everything was quiet and still. Until I heard a somewhat strangled, ragged breath.

Staring at her closed bedroom door, I stepped further into the living room and strained to listen to the muffled gasps on the other side. My mom took a breath, loud enough for me to hear and I took a few steps closer.

I hesitated to reach for the doorknob. My mom and I were both the suffer-in-silence type. It was a trait I'd learned from her when I was young, but you had to be dumb as a rock to not know why she was so upset, and shouldn't be alone. We'd both had a rough day, and if I was honest, we could probably both use some company.

Turning her bedroom doorknob, I peeked my head inside. My mom was tough, a hard-ass like no one I'd ever met. She pushed me when I was weak, which felt like all of the time, and she was a voice when the small, inconsequential town of Whitely didn't have one. Yet, when she forgot to be that pillar of strength everyone else needed, she could be soft and kind, even if I rarely saw it. And curled into a trembling heap on her bed, she looked just . . . miserable.

It wasn't me this time, weak and broken, the way it had been on so many other occasions.

"Mom," I whispered.

She sat up on her elbow and peered over her shoulder at me. Her eyes were red and her long hair fell in a dark, tangled cascade down her back. "Sophie . . ." She cleared her throat. "You should be in your room doing your homework." She blew into the tissue clutched in her hand and tucked her hair behind her ear. Even now, in front of me, she was trying to make herself presentable.

Instead of explaining, I crawled onto her bed beside her, into the spot where my dad rarely slept anymore and looked at her. She smelled of orange blossoms and vanilla, and even the smeared makeup beneath her lashes didn't dull her beauty. My mom was a lot of things, but she was smart and strong and beautiful, and my dad was an idiot. He'd pushed our Skype call back a couple hours and I'd only just realized the time. "Dad didn't call, did he?"

With a sigh, she blew her nose. "He's probably bombarded with custom party menus and last-minute requests."

She and I both knew that wasn't why he blew her off. The truth was we didn't even know if my dad really worked as much as he said he did. Sure, the money kept coming in, but that meant nothing. The whole reason we'd moved from Florida was so they could work on their marriage in a place with less temptation. So he would stay away from Clarice, the chef who taught him everything he knew . . . and more. Not that they'd told me that. The information I'd collected about my broken family had been from their late-night arguments behind closed doors and underhanded comments to one another at the dinner table, which they thought I was too naive to understand.

"Maybe," I said instead, but when her eyes met mine, her brow furrowed and she tilted her head. She knew I wasn't stupid, and for the first time, it was like she realized I wasn't just a kid anymore, and her eyes filled with tears again.

"It's okay, Mom," I breathed, and wrapped my arms around her shoulders as we lay back down on her bed, just as she'd done for me so many times. Like when I'd come home from school crying because the other kids were calling me Club Foot, or when I was so frustrated that I couldn't be just like everyone else—that I couldn't play like the other kids because of my leg braces.

She was hard on me, and overbearing most of the time, but whatever my mom's faults, I realized it was because of her that I hadn't felt shrunken and weak around others for a very long time. She pushed me to be stronger, and as irritating as it was, I knew a small part of me was.

For her sake, I wished my father cared half as much about appearances as she did.

"Your father's a jerk," she muttered, tempering her tone, though she didn't need to.

"He's an asshole, Mom—you can say it. A topnotch one at that."

She huffed a laugh, and I tightened my hold around her. I might've had a gut-wrenching day or two, but my mom had been going through much worse for years.

"I'm sorry," I whispered, squeezing my eyes shut as I breathed her in. After the past twenty-four hours, I could understand the fear she had for me—and not just teen pregnancy. It was everything that might come after it. And I knew in that moment that had I been pregnant, she wouldn't have disowned me. She wouldn't have done to me what her mother did to her. My mom was harsh, but she wasn't heartless. She would've done everything she could so that I wouldn't have to marry a man out of obligation, only to have him betray me over and over, like my dad had done to her.

She patted my arm and kissed my hand. "I'm sorry too."

SEVEN
ALEX

DAY 2
DECEMBER 8

I stared at my math homework sprawled out on the counter, knowing I wasn't going to get very far with the screaming headache settling into the base of my skull. It'd only gotten worse since I'd woken up, so it should've been a relief that class was cancelled again due to Mrs. Gunderson's kids being sick, but for the first time in my life, I was disappointed to have a day off school; being cooped up in the apartment with Jimmy was much worse.

Leaning my elbows on the table, I glanced at the math book sitting next to me and thought about Sophie. I hadn't really stopped thinking about her, actually. When she'd tried to explain why she needed the pregnancy test, I didn't care to listen, but the more I thought about the guy who should've been standing there with her instead of me, the more it pissed me off that he wasn't.

I wouldn't want my own kid sister to have to go through that alone, even if I feared she likely would. The truth was, I didn't know anything about her anymore, and I wanted her to know how incredibly sorry I was for that, and for what I'd done. Even if we were only related by marriage, she was my sister, and I was supposed to protect her, and whatever she might've thought about me, I hadn't forgotten about her. I'd even asked my grandma to help me find her, but she got too sick before she could. I would tell Kayla on my own though, when I was eighteen, after I found her myself.

I scrubbed my hands over my short hair and straightened on the rickety stool. Why was I worried about Sophie when I should've been worrying about the virus? It was starting to freak me out, and now that I felt half dead, I decided on taking the news warnings a bit more seriously.

At first, the outbreak coverage just added salacious bits in the news reports, something other than downed power lines and illegal poaching in the backcountry. Now that more and more people in this tiny town were getting sick, it actually felt real—like I was trapped in a damn fish bowl—and sleeping on a shitty couch didn't help the ache in my bones and neck.

At least the growing panic got Jimmy out of the house to take care of a quick job for the mayor, which he couldn't put off any longer. It was probably the only way I'd get to squeeze in some more sleep on the couch before he came back and took over the living room again.

Closing my math book, I rose to my feet. I was thirsty, but too tired to clean a dirty glass. Even if the worn leather couch had cushions so deflated I could feel the frame beneath me, it practically beckoned me to curl up for a quick nap.

Jimmy would be pissed I hadn't cleaned the apartment by the time he returned, but his wrath was nothing compared to the monster headache I needed to sleep away.

The leather creaked as I sat down with a satisfied groan, and I yanked my folded sleeping bag off the back of the couch and pulled it over me, hoping it would stave off the chill in the air.

When the McDonald's commercial ended and the news came back on, I unmuted the TV.

"—spreading panic, the CDC seems to be more quiet than expected," the woman anchor said. "There's been a lot of vague talk, but hopefully we'll know more after their official statement tomorrow in Atlanta. Meanwhile, the number of patients reported in Wales yesterday was staggeringly high as well, though the CDC isn't sure it's the same disease."

As much as I felt the need to listen to what they had to report, warmth seeped in around me, and as I let out a deep breath, the tension in my body began to ease. The exhaustion was suddenly overwhelming and sleep was so close, my thoughts became inconsequential as my mind began to blur.

I was on the cusp of blissful sleep when the door crashed open.

"Sleeping?" Jimmy growled, more ferocious than usual. He slammed the door behind him. "You're fucking sleeping? This place is a dump." He hit my feet off the couch, and I sat up with a lurch.

"Hey—it's not even my mess!" I shouted back, wishing he would crawl back into whatever hole he was born in and leave me the hell alone.

"I give you a place to sleep, and you help out around here. That was the damn deal." He dropped his tool bag onto the ground with a thud. His scowl was deeper than I'd seen before, and the shadows around his eyes were dark, like he hadn't slept in days, even if I knew that wasn't true.

"You said I could have a room," I reminded him. "I get a shitty old couch that smells like Cheetos—"

Jimmy growled, picked up a half-empty beer can, and sent it sailing across the room, hitting the far wall. It was a warning shot, I imagined. He was clearly pissed, even if he had no right to be. I wasn't his maid, and I cleaned up after myself all the time. He was the barbarian, not me. Sweat glistened on his forehead and beaded on his temples, and the veins in his eyes were so red I thought they might pop.

"Seriously, man. You look like hell. Are you—"

"You ungrateful piece of shit." Jimmy hurled one of his discarded boots at me, and it hit me in the face like a ten-pound brick.

I jumped to my feet. "What the fuck, man?" My surprise turned to fury, and then pain. It all sped through my veins as I brought my fingers to my bloody lips. Jimmy was a mean-looking guy with a semi-permanent snarl carved on his face, and he was definitely a bully and a dick, but this was the first time he'd been violent.

I balled my hands into fists. "Never do that again," I warned. My voice was so low, I wasn't sure I'd even said it. My chest heaved with a vehemence like nothing I'd ever felt before, and my head pounded with an overpowering exhaustion I couldn't shake.

"This building is infested with sickness," Jimmy spat. "For all I know, you're sick and you've been touching *everything.*" He stomped to the fridge to grab a beer. "Dirty, mangy kid—you're the reason my sister's dead! You're lucky I let you stay here at all." His words hurt a thousand times more than the shoe, and my vision began to blur. I clenched my teeth so tight, a pain shot through my jaw.

"I want this place cleaned up before I get out of the shower. You hear me, you little shit?" He pointed a crooked index finger at me.

I needed to get out of the apartment before things got out of my control.

"Ungrateful prick," he muttered again, and he disappeared into his bedroom, slamming the door shut behind him.

"Fuck you," I uttered, and grabbed my jacket off the back of the chair, then my beanie from the coffee table, and strode to the door. "It's your shit. You clean it up," I grumbled. I would not be his punching bag, especially not when it felt like I'd already been hit by a steamroller.

I slammed the front door shut behind me and stepped out into the hallway. *Screw this guy and this place.* I didn't need to deal with Jimmy. He could get his check, and I would sleep in the damn gym for four months if I had to. Anything was better than dealing with him.

Pulling my beanie over my head, I headed for the elevator and stopped short.

Sophie stood just outside the doors as they slid closed, long hair piled on top of her head. Her blue eyes were wide and fixed on me.

"Is everything okay?" she asked, shoving her cell phone back into her pocket. "You look . . . angry."

"I'm fine." I walked past her to press the down button. I didn't want to be rude, but I wasn't in the mood to chitchat either. The doors dinged back open, and I stepped inside.

"Hey, wait—" Sophie stepped into the elevator beside me, and I pressed the button for the lobby. "You're bleeding," she whispered, reaching for me. Her fingers brushed my cheek as she angled my face toward the halogen light above.

"I'm fine," I repeated, and my eyes shifted to hers, but I didn't pull away. Her fingers were warm and soft, and the scent of sunshine and clean linen wafted off her, which was strangely comforting.

"What happened?" She eyed my busted lip.

"I fell. Don't worry about it." I was *not* going to tell her Jimmy threw a shoe at me. There was enough pity in her eyes already. A shoe, of all things, was almost humiliating.

Sophie's hand dropped to her side. "I *am* worried about it," she said, more adamant than I'd expected.

"Trust me, it could've been worse." But that statement didn't help matters any. The creases in her brow intensified, and she looked almost angry. "Hey," I said more softly as the elevator shook, descending to the lobby. The last thing I needed was to see a girl's face crumple because she was worried about *me*. "It's fine —*I'm* fine. It was a stupid thing."

Sophie's gaze shifted over my face, and I could tell she was anxious for me. Through the exhaustion and frustration, her concern resonated in a way that made my chest ache a little. No one had ever looked at me like that, and oddly, unlike when strangers regarded me with pitying and judgmental stares after they learned anything remotely true about me, I liked that Sophie cared, even if I knew I wasn't worth a second thought. I liked her being so close I could smell the scent of her clean clothes and feel the heat coursing off her, warming the air around me.

I stared into the blue and yellow flecks of her eyes, and at the freckles dotting the bridge of her nose and dappling her cheeks. She was more than pretty. I felt a pull to her I'd never experienced with someone before. It was like there was a physical tether between us, shortening by the second.

I averted my gaze, and Sophie cleared her throat and took a step back. "Is there anything I can do to help?"

"No." I shook my head. "I just need some sleep. That couch is shit."

"You can sleep on my couch," she offered. "My mom won't mind if you need a place—"

"No," I told her. I was *not* a charity case. "Thanks though." Sophie had no idea who I was, neither did her mom. And if Sophie knew half of the shit I'd done, she wouldn't be offering or looking at me with so much concern.

"Seriously, Alex, I owe you—Oh! Here's the money for the tests—"

I brushed her proffered hand away, the pity in her eyes and in the strain of her voice making me feel even sicker. "Don't worry about it."

The door opened on the lower level, and my feet wouldn't move fast enough as I stepped into the lobby. I didn't want Sophie seeing me with a busted up lip anyway, and I needed space—I needed air. Besides, I was pond scum compared to her—the preppy, mayor's daughter who lived in the closest thing this town had to an ivory tower.

"Fine," she said softly. The hurt in Sophie's voice was unmissable though, and I remembered the fear I'd seen in her eyes only yesterday. Despite my irritation and exhaustion, I knew she wasn't a pretty pink princess like I wanted to believe, and she didn't deserve the cold shoulder.

Feeling like an ass, I turned around, about to ask her about the pregnancy test, when the elevator door closed again and she was gone.

"Damn." I closed my eyes and inhaled a deep, calming breath. I'd worry about Sophie's feelings after I found a dark corner in class to pass out in. For now, my face was throbbing, though the taste of blood was less noticeable. I just needed some real, uninterrupted sleep and I would be fine.

I rubbed the back of my neck and wished I could telepathically transport myself down the hall. Somehow that tiny wink of sleep had pulled me in so much I couldn't shake it, like with just the promise of it, my body required more.

As I headed down the hall toward the connection tunnel, the door to the clinic flew open and I stumbled back. A police officer stepped out. "You can't be down here," he said, knocking past me.

I bit back the acerbic words on my tongue as the officer hurried through the mayor's door, two offices down. The door to the clinic squeaked shut, but not all the way, and I could see crimson spattering the floor. I leaned forward in alarm, unable to resist, and another officer covered up a pair of sock-covered feet hanging over an exam table.

Blood. And vomit. A lot of it. All over the floor. I didn't do blood or vomit. The sneaking memories of my past billowed to mind, and I swallowed thickly, trying to keep the cereal I ate for breakfast down as I took an unsteady step backward. What the hell had happened? Was it the virus?

The other police officer stepped out next, his eyebrows drawn together and his lips pursed. "You can't be here, son—"

"Yeah, yeah," I grumbled, and turned to leave. "I'm going." Shoving my hands in my pockets, I headed for the lobby, uncertain where the hell I was going if I couldn't go to the school.

As I walked in front of the entry door, it swung open and a woman shoved into me, nearly knocking me on my ass. "What's with everyone?" I shouted. "Don't you see I'm walking here?" I bit back a few other superlatives, even if the woman was barely fazed.

She glanced at me, her green eyes wild with alarm, but I didn't think it was because of me. Her long, brunette hair was disheveled and hanging in her face, and she looked pale, but then so did a lot of people in Alaska. It's why people like me stood out so much. Was she sick or just rude and oblivious?

"They were here yesterday," she spat into the phone, then switched it to the right side, and I noticed a crown tattooed behind her left ear. "I had them do what you told me to—just like you'd said—now something's not right," she said, frantic. "*I'm* not right. Why is this happening—what's wrong with me?"

I registered the blood around her nose as she looked at me again, not really even seeing me, before she continued toward the elevator.

Another woman with burgundy hair hurried past me with a walkie-talkie gripped in her hand. The high pitch of radio static pierced the empty lobby, before the speaker clicked on. "It's coming into port now," a male voice said. "They don't care if we have the provisions or not."

"God damn it," she whispered, bringing the receiver to her mouth. She was about to speak when she noticed me watching her, dumb and a little fuzzy.

"You shouldn't be down here," she told me, and the scent of clean linen and oranges wafted off of her. I saw Sophie's slope nose in her features and the blue-and-yellow flecked eyes, and immediately knew she was Sophie's mom, the mayor. "There's about to be a horde of people in here. Go home—now."

"Fine," I said, throwing my hands up. I shoved the door open. I wasn't going home and apparently I wasn't staying in the lobby either. "Freeze to death it is," I barked out, and I nearly stumbled down the steps into the biting cold air of the afternoon. It felt like shards of ice pierced my flesh, but it was better than the worsening pain in the back of my head, the incessant throbbing, and the heat that flourished behind my ears and down into my throat.

The mountains surrounding Whitely were covered in white and were menacingly jagged against the gray afternoon sky. I wasn't sure where my feet were taking me, just that I had to keep moving and find somewhere to sleep before I passed out in the snow where I stood.

Blowing heat into my cupped hands, I eyed a boat graveyard and shrugged. I'd slept in worse. I forced my eyes to stay open and followed the road past the kayak center, but the longer I walked the fuzzier my mind became and the heavier my limbs felt against the cold wind.

As I shut my eyes against an abrasive gust, I almost forgot to open them again, and it was all I could do to keep upright and let my feet carry me wherever they would take me.

EIGHT
SOPHIE

As the elevator opened on the eighth floor again, I breathed a little easier knowing the pregnancy test had been taken out with the trash, but I wondered if Alex would be okay. I didn't know Jimmy very well, just that he always smelled like stale beer and aftershave and he wasn't very good at his job—or so my mom always said. It was hard enough to think of him as an adult, let alone a parental figure, but I hoped he wasn't violent. I had a feeling Alex didn't just fall; he didn't strike me as a clumsy guy.

I eyed Jimmy's apartment door as I walked past, expecting to hear the snarl of a rabid dog inside—but I heard a crash instead, then another one, like he was upturning furniture—and I hurried more quickly down the hall. At least I knew Alex wasn't inside.

Forcing myself to focus, I blew out a fortifying breath and made my way toward Jesse's apartment three doors down. Sweat beaded my brow the entire way. I wasn't sure why I was so apprehensive to see Jesse, so much so that I'd lingered on the fourth floor, staring longingly at Bailey's place for nearly an hour, like magically she'd walk out and say hello. I still hadn't heard back from her either.

When I arrived at apartment 808, I stood in front of the door for a few heartbeats, wondering how sick Jesse actually was. He still hadn't texted me back, but his mom had answered when I'd called their main line this morning. While Mrs. Phillips didn't seem particularly happy I was bothering her, at least I knew Jesse was alive—sick and in bed, but alive. Even if I couldn't see him, at least he'd know I came by.

I knocked on the door and listened for footsteps on the other side. I could hear the low chatter of what sounded like the television, but there were no rustling sounds or creaking floors inside. I was about to knock again when I heard a cough. A spring squeaked, and finally, the door cracked open. Air wafted through the opening, so acerbic I swallowed involuntarily. Then Mrs. Phillips's bloodshot eyes and green-tinted skin came into view.

She opened the door further, and I took a step back. Her blonde and gray-streaked hair was oily and matted to her round cheeks, and her blue eyes looked almost like they were fogged over— fogged over and narrowed on me, holding no kindness.

"What is it, Sophie?" Her voice rattled with phlegm like it was suspended in her throat.

I swallowed thickly, unable to resist, and forced myself to breathe. "I'm sorry, Mrs. Phillips. I thought I would see if Jesse—"

"I told you, Jesse is sick."

"But—I mean, can I bring you guys anything?"

"Go away, Sophie." She slammed the door in my face, and with it came a wave of blood-burning fear. She looked near death, smelled like it too, and if she was as bad as that, Jesse probably was too. Maybe he was even worse. *And I'd written him off.*

Guilt sank heavy and deep in my gut, and I shuffled back down the hall toward the elevator, gripping my churning stomach the whole way. The scent of Mrs. Phillips was nauseating and seared the inside of my nose.

If school was cancelled because Katie's kids were sick, and if

Jesse and his mom were sick—as well as Henry and Sarah and the others visiting the clinic yesterday, it was hard to refute that the virus was here. A different sort of flu seemed like wishful thinking.

I nearly broke into a run. Was I next or did I already have it?

I shook my head as I pushed the elevator open. I already knew the answer, didn't I? I'd felt sick for a couple days, and even if I didn't feel as sick as Mrs. Phillips looked, it was the only logical explanation. Or had it really been the stress of my first, and definitely last, pregnancy scare? Part of me wanted to go down to the first floor and find my mom, but I knew she had her own shit to deal with. She'd called the divorce lawyer this morning and started her morning off with fresh tears. And if I was wrong and I wasn't sick, she didn't need to worry about me on top of everything else. She already did that enough as it was. I would wait until she got home tonight and tell her if I wasn't feeling better.

I stepped into the elevator and hit the button for the tenth floor, hoping the fear and nausea that lingered from smelling Mrs. Phillips would pass or at least hold out until I got home, so I could puke in my toilet. I'd feel better after that.

And if I didn't? I would call my mom.

The two floors up felt like nine, and I nearly wept with relief when the double doors finally popped opened, and I shot out into the hallway.

"Hold the door!" a woman shouted.

I stumbled back inside to hold the button, and glanced down the hallway to find a woman I didn't recognize—I assumed a medic—wheeling a stretcher out from the apartment next to mine, at the end of the hall. Briefly, I questioned where the hell she'd come from and why I didn't recognize her, but I didn't have much time to wonder because, for the second time in mere minutes, I swallowed the bile rising in my throat.

A person was splayed out on the stretcher rolling down the hallway toward me. Long, slender fingers gripped the side of it. It was JJ, it had to be. Hers was the only apartment down the hall from mine.

Her body strained against a convulsion, and she began thrashing and coughing before she lurched upright. Blood splattered her clothes, and her green eyes were wide and circled with red.

"It'll be all right," the medic insisted, trying to lay JJ back down onto the stretcher. The woman had blonde hair in a haphazard braid down her back. "Just hold on!"

I jumped out of the way as the medic wheeled JJ closer. JJ was *not* going to hold on; she was coughing up blood—it was everywhere. Her arms flailed as she convulsed again, the gurney creaking and rattling as she struggled against it. Blood gurgled from between her lips and trickled down the side of her face and back over her crown tattoo, just below her ear. It wasn't black anymore; it wasn't even red—it was a muddled brown of bile and blood.

The elevator doors dinged, like they were about to close, and I threw my arm out to bounce them open again before jumping into the hall, out of the way as much as I could be.

JJ thrashed again, choking and gasping for air, and I covered my mouth to stifle a scream. The stretcher slammed into the back of the elevator and the medic hit the lobby button.

As the doors began to close, JJ reached out, her hand splayed like she was reaching for me, and her eyes met mine. They weren't green anymore, but red with blood, and she hissed like she was trying to say something.

I choked back a sob as the elevator shut her inside and the hallway fell silent.

I stood motionless in horror. Then my body began to quake. Lightness filled my mind, and my stomach sprang into another somersault. In a frenzy, I ran for my apartment on wobbly legs. My key card beeped angrily at me, then beeped again before the lock clicked, and I shoved the door open. It slammed against the wall as I barely made it to the bathroom. Falling to my knees, I heaved. As my body retched and fear seemed to swallow whole every coherent thought I had, I prayed what happened to JJ wouldn't be my fate.

57

NINE
SOPHIE

My stomach lurched, and I squeezed my eyes closed as I breathed in through my nose. The vomiting. The aching. It was all I could do to take a sip of ginger ale and keep it down. That was supposed to help when you had the flu, right? I'd tried to eat a cracker, but it came roaring back up almost immediately.

I dialed my mom's cell for the seventh time, and again it rang until her voicemail clicked on. I hung up and tried her work phone. "Come on, Mom," I rasped. I needed her. But like the first time I'd tried calling her office, it was busy. *She* was busy. With JJ? With the council meeting? It was probably about the virus, and I was afraid to turn on the television to find out what was happening. I didn't want a confirmation that what had happened to JJ would also happen to me.

I tucked the blanket higher around my neck and sank further into the couch. I wasn't sure if the foul feeling in the depths of my stomach was from the flu or an effect of JJ's blood-rimmed eyes, which I couldn't stop thinking about. Fear had a physical effect—if I'd learned anything in the past couple days. And even though I knew better than to let it get the better of me, how could I not fear what I'd seen?

I squeezed my eyes shut and tried to control each inhale and exhale. In through my nose: long and deep. Out through my mouth: steady, thoughtful, and controlled.

It had been three hours since the medic took JJ away on the stretcher. Three hours of intermittent, unsteady pacing back and forth as I tried to gather the nerve to step into the elevator and go down to see my mom. She'd likely heard what happened to JJ and would know if she was okay. She'd know what to do to make me feel better. My mom had a remedy for everything, even when I didn't want it. This time, though, I wanted it. I needed her to tell me I would be okay.

But the elevator . . . It was my only option down. I was too nauseous and wobbly to take ten flights of stairs, and I'd hurl before I got halfway down. Fear. Sickness. Whatever was living inside me was taking its toll, and the past thirty-six hours without much food was starting to catch up with me.

I peeled my heavy eyelids open and tried not to think about what I would find in the elevator or worry which parts of JJ might be splattered on the walls.

I held my breath, waiting for a wave of nausea to settle again, and clung to the desperate hope that JJ had survived whatever that was. If she was okay, even so close to death as she seemed, then I would be too. Mrs. Phillips would be okay, and Jesse.

With a slow blink, I stared at the soft glow of Christmas lights wrapped around the window. When I was little, we decorated a lot more than a few strings of lights. But our decorating tradition had dwindled over the years, resulting in untangling only a few strands on Thanksgiving and calling it good. Until now, I never missed our family time together. Where was my dad? He should be here with his family and not off with someone else, living a life that didn't have us in it.

Tears burned the backs of my eyes, and I choked out a sob.

What's happening? The news reports hadn't said the flu was anything like what I'd seen. Had they? My mind was so fuzzy, I wasn't sure of much anymore.

Unfurling myself from my blanket, I walked over to the living room window and pulled back the curtain. The sky had darkened, and night settled in blotting out the gloomy day. I'd never thought Whitely was a scary place but it suddenly seemed terrifying. Where would they have taken JJ? To Anchorage? Seward? Everything was so far away I wasn't sure she'd make the hour drive in either direction.

The lights of the harbor flickered amidst the falling snow, and though it was barely five in the evening, the world felt darker and colder than usual. A cruise ship, docked at the deep-water pilings down at the mouth of the sound, sent an unexpected wave of chills over my skin. What was it doing here? We didn't get tourist ships in port in the dead of winter.

A blur of movement caught my attention, and squinting, I could just make out a caravan of lights moving toward me. The closer they drew, the more I could make out a half dozen snowmobiles. They were traveling fast, and headed for the apartment building.

Heart racing, I dropped my phone onto the couch and trudged to the shoe cubby by the door to grab my Ugg boots. I leaned against the wall to steady myself as I tugged them on, dropping my right shoe as I almost fell over, then more adamantly tugged it on. It was all I could do to stay upright as my ponytail swung into my face, nearly throwing me off kilter again. My heavy, thick hair was more annoying than usual, and I growled as I made one last heave to get my other foot into my boot before it fell to the floor.

Flinging the door open as quickly as I could, I hurried toward the elevator, resolved to push another wave of nausea away and make it down to the first floor to see my mom before it was too late. I hesitated at the elevator, but only for a second before I pushed the button down.

The seconds were excruciatingly long, but finally, the doors opened. When a flash of red caught my attention, I closed my eyes and stepped inside, turning around as quickly as I could, only opening my eyes enough to see the panel in front of me. After pressing the lobby floor button, I squeezed my eyes shut, breathing through my nose to quell my hysteria as I prayed the elevator wouldn't stop until it got to the bottom.

TEN
ALEX

I dreamed of darkness in sweltering heat. Of heated metal searing through my skin so acute I imagined a knife slicing me from the back of my head down to the base of my spine. It was agonizing. Gashing. The feeling was what nightmares were made of if you feared dull knife blades, like I did. It felt like hundreds of them pierced my skin, and every heartbeat made the pain bolder, swelling to a blistering burn.

I'd seen death, but in a wakeful sleep—conscious, yet unable to open my eyes—it was alarmingly close. And a hauntingly familiar darkness pulled me in even further.

The recognizable scents of burning plastic and something inexplicably noxious filled my nostrils, sharp and astringent in the back of my throat. I pulled the bottom of my pajamas over my exposed, little feet, and swallowed the fear back down.

"Perra estúpida." The deep hiss of an inebriated voice lingered in my fitful dreams. His rage hummed in the oppressive heat of the upstairs, filling the hall closet where I hid. The hoarding, the dank scent of uncleanliness; it was like homecoming and a death sentence at once—hair-raising and grossly memorable.

I heard her whimper. "I didn't—"

"Cállate! One thing I asked, Maria. You want the whole fucking town to know what we're doing in here? Is that why you keep drawing attention?"

Shadows played beneath the closet door. "No, mi amor. Alejandro—it was Alejandro—he was outside playing—"

There was a thump and scuffle, and I cringed knowing her shriek would follow. My insides churned and twisted. My blood burned.

"Worthless puta . . ." On the nights my stepfather was angry, the demon inside him would grow tired before my mother was too far gone. But on the nights he was angry like this—and in another world—there was no stopping him until the frenzied rage was satisfied; until she was nothing more than a trembling heap on the floor that might not move for days.

My little sister began to cry in our bedroom. Though her voice was muffled, and the door closed, I worried he'd move on to her next.

My mother shrieked.

One fleshy thunk followed another, and my chin trembled, my body shaking just as violently.

They wanted Kayla and me out of their hair as much as possible—outside day or night, it didn't matter which. What they didn't want was my bringing the kids down the street to play at our house—a rule I never forgot, for my mother's sake, but the neighborhood kids didn't always understand. They didn't know what would happen, like I did. They didn't know the kitchen was off limits, or how it would be if my stepfather knew they'd been there.

"Worthless—"

A shriek filled my ears again.

With little hands balled into fists, shaking with panic and fury, I turned the knob and pushed the closet door open with all of my might, screaming and snarling as hot tears streamed down my face.

Hard wood hit sinewy muscle, and I fell back onto the pile of garbage bags I'd cocooned myself within as my stepfather shouted, not with rage this time, but with fear. His cry echoed in my head, descending with one deafening crash after another, followed by a final crunch.

I scrambled to my feet and peered down the stairs in awe. Red smeared the dingy wallpaper like sled marks in the snow, and my stepfather's body was unnaturally twisted. A dark puddle soaked the threadbare carpet beneath his head. He wasn't moving.

Relief flooded through me like warm water on a cool day. I basked in it, not fully certain what I'd done, but he'd stopped shouting and my mother had stopped shrieking. I looked at her with an unexpected sense of pride that instantly vanished when I saw her face.

"No—" she gasped, seizing hold of my arm. Her sharp fingernails dug into my flesh as she tried to hold herself steady, and rose to her knees. Her eye was swollen shut and bleeding.

"Stupid hijo," she rasped, and climbed to her feet. She pushed me aside, back into the closet, as she scrambled past me. "Que hiciste—" My mother's weak legs gave out, and she practically tumbled down the stairs after my stepfather.

"Mama—" Kayla cracked opened the bedroom door, sobbing.

"Go back inside!" I told her. "Go—"

"What have you done!" my mother squealed. Her screams came hard and fast as she pleaded for him to wake up, and for God to take me instead.

Foghorns echoed in the distance and wind lapped at my skin, making me shudder.

I tried to open my eyes—I needed to move—but my mind and body were leaden with sleep. I could only doze in an inferno that felt like it was melting me from the inside.

This is how I would die.

This was the end; my mother would get her final wish.

ELEVEN

SOPHIE

The ride down was painfully slow as the floor number changed from four to three, then two to one, until I finally reached the bottom. The elevator doors slid open and a blast of arctic air hit me. The entry doors were propped open, and shouts emanated all the way down the hall.

"Single file!" a man called from the entrance. I glanced back to find two men in reflective vests, ushering a group of people inside and pointing them toward the tunnel that led to the school. A dozen people entered, shaking and wrapped in snow-dusted jackets. One man had a toddler in his arms that didn't look like it was even moving.

They hurried past me, oblivious as I stood there waiting for them to pass.

"Follow the hall down to the right!" one of the ushers shouted, and pointed with his flashlight, though it was barely visible in the overhead lights.

Utter fear consumed me as I realized they were the people from the ship. None of them looked familiar, and *all* of them were potentially sick.

"Mom," I breathed, wrapping my arms around myself. All

nausea was forgotten, replaced with a dread unlike any I'd ever felt before. None of this was a good sign.

I headed down the hall behind the group, not dumb or curious enough to follow, but to check my mom's office a few doors down.

"Mom," I said, louder this time, and my legs moved more quickly. The municipal offices came into view and I practically ran to her open doorway. "Mom—"

She was at her desk and on the landline, just as I'd hoped. Her perfectly primped hair was tossed up in a messy ponytail, away from her face, and her tailored pantsuit was wrinkled.

"I don't care, Frank!" She gestured wildly. "I need you to get me—" She cursed under her breath as he cut her off. She was clearly frazzled—her skin ashen with exhaustion, or maybe it was worry—and she looked defeated in a way I'd never seen before. But, she was okay.

"Just—call me when you know something." She slammed the phone into the cradle, and dropped her head into her hands.

"Mom?"

She glanced at me and her blue eyes widened. "Sophie—"

"I saw the people coming in from the cruise ship."

"I know," she said as she stood up, steering me back out the door. "But you need to go home."

"Is this all because of the flu?"

"Yes, it is. That's why you need to go back up." She picked up a clipboard off her desk. The sheet of paper it held had a slew of names scribbled on it. *Symptoms and Quarantine Area* were written at the top of two columns; names were scribbled throughout—names I knew were crossed off the list. I gulped what little air I could manage.

"Do what I say." My mom gripped my arm. "Do not leave the apartment, Sophie. Do you understand me? This virus is spreading, and I don't want you to get it."

I already did, I was about to tell her, but bile rose up my throat and I tried to swallow it down. "Mom, is what happened to JJ going to happen to me? Is she okay?"

"Tessa." A voice rattled through the walkie-talkie. "You better get down here. There's a—" She turned down the volume dial on the device.

"Mom—"

"You have to go upstairs, Sophie." Her voice was thin and laced with desperation. "Please." Her eyes shimmered, and the fear in them told me this wasn't going to get better anytime soon. "It's not safe down here, not right now."

Whatever minute grasp I had on composure dissolved, and my vision blurred with tears. "Then come home with me. I don't want you to get it."

"I can't leave all of these people, Sophie. I'm taking precautions, I promise. I need you to be safe in the house, though, so that I don't worry about you." Her gaze bored through me, willing me to understand, and she pointed toward the elevator.

I nodded because her tone commanded me to, but I couldn't make my feet move to turn around as she headed out the door. I'd never seen her so scared and unkempt. "Mom—"

"Sophie, now!" she said, raising her voice. "Before the police see you. They are quarantining everyone down here into the gymnasium with the people off the ship, do you understand? Nearly everyone on the first five floors is already sick. I don't want them to see you down here—I do *not* want you to be locked in there with them until they can get things under control."

It wasn't as bad as I thought. It was worse. "What if they can't?" I blurted. "What if none of this is going to get better?" My thoughts spun as the horror seeped in, pulling me to the brink of hysteria. "I don't want to—"

"They're sending help," she told me, and grabbed my arm. "I promise. I'll be up soon, but this conversation is pointless if you get caught down here, okay?" The doors to the elevator opened again, and she tugged me inside. "Come on now, we have to be smart . . . We have to protect ourselves." Her words sounded rehearsed and empty, like she'd said them a million times or didn't believe them at all—I wasn't sure which.

"But Mom," I tugged away from her. "I'm *already* sick." I could barely force the words out.

"No," she said in a rush. "No, you're not." She pressed the elevator button so the doors would close. "Lock yourself in the apartment—don't open the door for anyone but me."

"Mom." My voice was barely audible. It was all too horrifying to be real. "Mom, I'm scared."

"Good, then listen—it's the only way." Her nostrils flared, and she pulled me into her arms, the elevator doors bumping against us before they opened again. "I love you, Sophie. I need you to do this for me, please." It was a plea, a desperate request, and even though I wanted to stay with her, I didn't want to disappoint her either.

"I don't want to leave you," I cried, tears dripping down my cheeks.

I could feel her body trembling as much as mine, the heat of her enveloping me as she squeezed her arms tighter. "I know, but it's only for a little while. I need to know what they're doing down here, so I can keep us safe." With a final squeeze, she slowly pulled away.

Her watery gaze was imploring and her chest heaved. She waited for me to understand.

Unable to, I nodded. I didn't want to be a burden when she was in the middle of so much danger.

"Now, please go. Keep warm and stay safe until I can get there —it's only until help comes," she promised again, with a smile. "And try to reach your father, and tell him we're safe." She wiped the moisture from beneath her eyes. "I love you."

"I love—"

"There is a mandatory quarantine. Everyone is to remain in

their own apartment . . ." Someone's nasally voice came over the intercom.

Eyes wide, my mom mouthed, "Go," and then the doors shut between us, and she was gone.

I didn't care about the blood on the floor around me. Fear and despondency gutted me as I rode the elevator to the tenth floor. Sobs ripped through me as I realized my mom's hug felt more like a goodbye, and as the doors opened, I reached for the first-floor button to go back down to her then I tumbled to my knees.

Whatever was happening to me, it was too late.

TWELVE
SOPHIE

DAY 3
DECEMBER 9

Fleetingly, my consciousness returned with the bright light of the bathroom boring into my brain. I forced my eyes open against their will. I was shaking and cold, despite my clothes, and suffocating in the stench of vomit. It was a smell I'd become so familiar with that I hadn't noticed at first.

A scream pierced the air and my heavy eyelids pulled themselves open again. Was it the TV? Another scream echoed from somewhere, more distant this time.

Beyond the haze, in the back of my mind some place, I knew I should be afraid, but it was all I could do to keep my eyes open amidst the fever. It was finally here, right in the base of my throat, and alive and coiling in my stomach.

I couldn't remember how I'd gotten here, and I had no idea how long I'd been curled up on the floor with my insides sour and burning, like lemon juice on a fresh wound.

With a groan, I flushed the toilet, uncertain how anything could still be coming out of me, and searched for the strength to climb to my feet. It felt nearly impossible, but somehow I managed as the world spun around me. I clutched the edge of the counter, then leaned into the doorframe to steady myself.

Bed. I needed my soft bed for my aching bones.

I stumbled out of the bathroom, bracing myself against the wall as I staggered into my bedroom—it was blissfully dark and welcoming. I could hear voices somewhere in the distance, down the hall, in the apartment next door. They seemed to be nowhere and everywhere all at once, but I couldn't be bothered to care. My clothes hurt my skin. The imperfections in the carpet cut into the bottoms of my feet. My head felt like a splitting rock.

I lingered in my bedroom doorway to catch my breath. I'd never been so tired in my life; I could barely think. I had been worried about something, something important, but I couldn't remember what it was.

Resting my head against the cool doorframe, I pried my eyes open. The sight of my bed brought tears to my eyes. I wanted to sleep forever and never wake up.

Forcing myself to keep moving, I took a step forward and stumbled, my knees hitting the floor with an explosive pain that shot its way through my legs.

With a weak cry, I grabbed at my comforter and strained to pull my upper body high enough to fall onto the mattress so I could rest. I heard a crash in the apartment below me, but I only got so far as peeling off my vomit-covered pants before everything faded to darkness once again.

THIRTEEN
ALEX

**TWO DAYS LATER
DECEMBER 11**

My grandmother lay weak and permanently attached to an oxygen machine in a hospital bed as her milky, green eyes blinked slowly up at me. They'd always been my comfort—my reassurance that everything would be okay.

"Did you eat the casserole I left you?" she rasped, worrying about me, even with her final few breaths. "It's potato and bacon . . . your favorite."

Tears welled in my eyes, but I forced a wavering smile and nodded. "Yeah, I did." I didn't have the heart to tell her that had been weeks ago, she just didn't realize it.

She tried to reach for my face, but her hand trembled in midair and she dropped it onto her chest. She was the only good thing left in my life, and I could see the life force she clung to fading before my eyes. What was I going to do without her?

I took her soft, wrinkly fingers in mine, waiting for the warmth in her body to return. Willing her to stay with me just a little bit longer. "Don't go, Abuela," I pleaded. "Please." Since my moth-

72

er's death, and Kayla being taken away to live with a different family, my grandma was all I had left. All composure I'd held onto for the past week was gone the moment the doctor told me it was time to say goodbye.

Even if I'd known this moment would come—and knew she could never take me in because her health was so bad—I prayed she would stay with me until I could become the man she always said I would be, until she could see it for herself. "Please . . ." I lowered my forehead to her arm and cried. "I need you."

"No, mijo. You are strong." She paused to draw in a strangled breath. "And you are good—"

I shook my head with a sob, knowing that wasn't true. I'd killed my mother by killing my stepfather, even if he was a monster. I'd gotten my half sister taken away—I didn't even know where she was. What if her foster family was as mean as mine?

Without my grandma I had no one left, and I didn't want to go back to the cage the Smiths kept me in—a corral, but for kids. I'd already run away from them once, from the small room that felt like a prison I was only released from for chores and school. I didn't want to be locked away. I didn't want to live with strange people anymore. I wanted to be here, with her, forever.

"Alejandro," my grandma said more brusquely. "Look at me." Her oxygen machine beeped, and she had to clear her throat. Her voice was a phlegmy veil of goodbyes, and I couldn't bear to listen. "Look at me," she said more slowly, commanding me to listen.

Forcing myself to meet her gaze, I lifted my head, staring at the blurry outline of her face.

She smiled. "You are so strong, mijo," she said, drawing in another arduous breath. "You, of all people, will be fine without me."

"No," I whispered, sniffling back tears. Why did no one ever stay?

"Mijo," she said softly, her eyebrows lifting in a plea of their own. "You are almost thirteen. You will be old enough to make

your own decisions soon, but you must be good. Be kind. Be strong. One day you will have a good life and people who love you. I know you will."

I shook my head, my chin quivering. She said that all the time, but everyone always left. My mom. My real father. Kayla was gone and it was all my fault. Now my abuela was leaving me too.

Metal clanked on metal, and the distant ding of buoys on the harbor filled the crisp air around me. Sea birds called, and power lines hummed somewhere close by as I peeled my eyes open.

The dull, steely-gray sky cast swaying shadows in the whistling breeze, and two-by-fours lined the ceiling above me. Life jackets hung from hooks on the cement walls, and a sharp pain shot through my ears and temples as I lifted my head. My eyes were wet, my mouth dry, and my throat felt like sandpaper as I tried to swallow. I was pretty sure a seabird had crawled into my mouth while I was sleeping and died.

When my grandma's face flashed to mind, I glanced at the skylights trying to remember where I was, and how I'd gotten there. All I could recall was being cold in the flames of a fire.

Sitting up on a pile of blankets, I gazed down from a rickety boat carcass that shimmied each time I moved and onto a grease-stained floor in the empty warehouse. There were three bays with vehicle lifts—maybe for boats, and exhaust puffed from a truck's tailpipe, rumbling just outside the roll-up door.

I wasn't the only one here.

I licked my lips—trying to determine if I was apprehensive, caught in a place I didn't belong or recognize, or if I was indifferent—because water was all that mattered. I was dehydrated, and the person who owned the truck idling outside might be able to help me.

I wasn't sure how long I'd been unconscious, only that the incandescent sun was now rising just above the cloud-dusted mountains in the south. I peered down at my sullied jacket and mud-crusted gloves, confused. Only vaguely did I remember crawling. Where and for how long I couldn't recall, but I'd wanted to die—that part I remembered clearly.

I pulled off my tattered beanie and rubbed my hand over my head.

I'd had dreams of my stepfather, lying dead on the floor at the foot of the stairs. I saw my mother hovering over him, and recalled her crumpled body on the kitchen floor only days after—the stench of vomit, the pool of blood surrounding her. I remembered the guilt and confusion I'd felt. Now I felt anger as the memories flourished from a faint flicker, previously pushed to the back of my mind, to resentment. I thought I'd died somewhere between my dreams and now, and still the past was there, breathing down my neck like a hungry dragon.

Rubbing my face, I forced my eyes to stay open—to wake up and get out of the warehouse. All that mattered was water.

I clung to the ledge of the boat and winced as I pulled myself to my feet, trying to stay as quiet as I could so I wouldn't alarm anyone who might be around. My body didn't want to move, it protested with every infinitesimal movement, but I had no choice.

The instant I jumped out of the boat and my feet touched the cold cement, I regretted it. A biting chill and sharp pain shot through my heel and up my leg. "Sweet Mary . . ."

One footstep at a time, I made it to the roll-up door. I probably should've cared more that someone would see me, but I hadn't done anything wrong, at least not that I knew of.

Hesitating at the door, I squinted into the cab of the Dodge, trying to make out any people inside. Through the soft glow of the muted morning reflected on the glass, it looked empty. I stepped around the truck and took a few eager steps into the wind. My feet dragged a little, but that was fine with me. Snow surrounded me, the closest thing to water I was going to get, and I lowered to my knees beside a mound of freshly fallen snow. It was pristine and white, and I shoved a handful of snow into my mouth. The moisture seeped into every dry crevice, instantly reviving my tongue.

My throat felt frozen as I swallowed it down, but at least it was wet. Snow had never tasted so good, and I bit into another handful, ignoring the numbness that followed and the cold burn in my nose. I reveled in every blissful moment.

The morning was glacially cold, like the harbor itself had frozen over—not just the mountains around Whitely—and the wind was harsher than I anticipated, though I wasn't certain why. Alaska was a bitch when she wanted to be, no matter where you were. In the dirty city streets, in the open wild—even out here in a cove of picturesque perfection—everything was always a test.

Enjoying the last of the melting snow in my mouth, I grounded myself to the familiar brine in the air, inherent in these seaside towns. I was by the pier, across the street from the Heston Building —the barracks toward the edge of the town. Whitely wasn't a big city, but after the night I'd had and the missing hours of who knew what, I didn't feel like walking the mile or so back to the apartment complex. Plus, a storm was coming in.

I stared out at the impending gray and wondered where the Dodge's driver was. I had half a mind to use their truck if they weren't going to, but I imagined that wouldn't go over well. A faraway voice in my head reminded me that I didn't care.

I climbed back up to my feet and squinted into the bright sheen of snow a few yards away. Just beyond the Dodge's front bumper was a mound with a familiar outline.

Taking a few hesitant steps closer, I told myself my luck was not this bad. I was not going to stumble upon a dead body here, in Whitely of all places.

But I was wrong.

Eyes wide, I glanced furtively around. I would've guessed frostbite or maybe a heart attack by the look of the man's age, but he had a handgun gripped in his blue fingers. Why was he holding a gun? I didn't see any blood-stained snow, and it didn't look like there had been a struggle, but I wasn't a CSI, and I had no idea what the hell had happened.

No one was out here, save for a dead man and me. No one to tell the authorities what had happened or that I hadn't done anything wrong. Even if I knew they couldn't pin this on me, I worried they'd try. Not that I'd ever been tagged a murderer, but I knew how things worked in places like this. When shit happened in inconsequential towns like Whitely, the authorities started looking for strange coincidences, and a new kid with a laundry list of petty crimes would be enough for them to dive deeper and question everything about me. And whether I liked it or not—*accidental* or not—I'd been associated with both of my parents' deaths, and I began to spiral.

"Shit!" I grabbed my head and I nearly stumbled back as my eyes shifted around the white expanse. There were abandoned cars and shipping containers further down the shore, but there were no other close vehicles, no people, or other bodies that I could see. There were no bear tracks in the snow. What the hell was he protecting himself from?

The truck engine began to peter out, and I realized the old man must've been there for hours, maybe longer—the truck running for just as long. He'd been running from something or someone, but there was no way in hell I was sticking around to find out the rest.

With wide, determined steps, I headed for the apartment complex. I'd tell them what I found, even if I wasn't sure how I would answer when they asked me what I was doing out here. *I can't remember* was *not* an option. Getting away from Jimmy, that was close enough to the truth.

I hadn't taken a dozen steps, imagining an anonymous call to the police might be an alternative solution, when I heard a moaning cry drift toward me in the wind. My body stilled and the hair on the back of my neck stood up—I could practically feel it reaching for safety. The cry came again, and it sounded small but was penetrating, much like a seagull's cry pierced the sea air. It was more human than that though.

I gazed up at the rundown barracks across the street. It was a lonely, godforsaken place. You would have to hold me at gunpoint to get me to go in, but the cry emanating from inside was almost like a ghost, luring me closer. I glanced back at the old man, his outline barely visible. Maybe he hadn't been alone.

The hair rose on the back of my arms this time. I thought it might be a trick—why, I wasn't sure—but some delinquent teens could've been playing inside, fucking with me. *But I'm in Whitely.* I was sure I'd met just about all of the teens in this place, and I couldn't imagine Jeannie inside, playing a prank like that on me. And there was still the old man's body to consider.

The cry met my ears again, and sounded so small and so scared, I thought it might be a child or a frightened girl.

Fleetingly, I thought of Sophie.

There was another despondent moan, and my heart raced faster.

I had to think fast, someone could be injured or dying inside.

Or someone was being hurt.

There was no way to know what I was walking into, and I wasn't stupid enough to go in empty handed. Against my better judgement, I hurried back for the old man's gun. He'd been worried about something enough to carry it; I'd be signing my death certificate by ignoring my gut and going in there at all, let alone unarmed.

I eyed the pistol, trying to ignore the intermittent crying. I could've run back to the apartments a mile or so away to get someone else to help whoever was inside, but deep down, I knew this was on me. By the time I could get someone else to check it out, it might be too late, and I would have to live with that. I wasn't sure I could take being the cause of any more death.

"Fuuuck," I growled, and pried the gun from the man's frost-bitten fingers. I was definitely going to regret this.

FOURTEEN
ALEX

Heart thrumming, and nerve endings wired and firing like never before, I slowed just outside the behemoth-sized building built of cement and steel, and peered up at the boarded and broken windows. White puffs of air dispersed around my face as I listened. I could hear the wind whistling through the halls, but there was no more crying. The coward in me hoped I was only hearing things.

Just when I'd half-convinced myself my imagination was simply fettered with ghost stories about this place, another cry echoed from a couple of stories up. I knew in my gut it was a child, and a new, desperate fear took over.

I stared down at the gun, realizing it would only scare a kid. I released the magazine to count the bullets. It was important to know what I had in case I needed to use it, even if only as a warning shot to scare someone or something away. I felt a pang of regret amidst a wave of relief; there were no bullets—the damn thing wasn't even loaded.

I tossed the empty magazine aside and ran for a doorless entry at the end of the building a dozen yards away, the gun gripped tightly in my hand. I prayed it would be menacing enough if I needed it to be, and that the day would end with my feeling like a good Samaritan, not filled with regret or worse.

Determined, I stepped through a busted glass door and into the building's dark corridor, where I was hit instantly with the dank scent of mold. Even if I could see patches of light through the windows along the building, the darkness in between was more ominous than I was comfortable with. I peered to the left and then to the right. By the look of the outside, the building was a few stories tall, with a hundred rooms at least to house a garrison of soldiers. And other than the need to find a staircase leading up, I had no idea which way to go. Preferring more light than darkness, I started down the hall to the right.

The passageway was narrow and cluttered with debris. Weather-ravaged and rotted, the walls were tagged with graffiti and had begun to crumble, and the floors were wet with puddled snow. Each footstep echoed as I tried not to step too clumsily around uprooted tiles and deteriorated stone. Rusted piping lined the ceiling, and old wiring from the overhead lights swung in the wind. Loose glass rattled in window frames, and old doors squeaked in unison with a distant drip.

My body was aching. I was hungry. Thirsty. Exhausted. But none of it matched the fear I felt standing in a place that screamed, *run*.

My knuckles tightened around the gun grip as I peered through an open door, into what looked like a hospital room in my search for the stairs. Rusted bed frames were stacked in the far right corner, and moss grew up the walls. I didn't want to know what had happened in this place—in a military hospital—so I moved on to the next door, petrified by the thought of what might jump out at me.

But despite the horror of what *would* happen in Stephen King's world, the rooms were mostly empty and all of them the same: dirty, chilly, and hauntingly disturbing.

Warnings to turn back were scribbled on the walls, and Led Zeppelin insignias overlapped what I assumed were hex symbols. Everything was eerie and equally warped by the elements. Vintage office chairs were scattered around, and a few moth-eaten uniforms that looked like they were from another time were discarded in a random pile on the floor. I passed a mess hall and a theater with dozens of torn seats facing a wall of peeling paint. Then another moaning cry drifted toward me.

I squinted, barely able to make out a flight of stairs at the end of the hall. I walked faster, debating if I should call out and tell whoever was crying that I was there to help, and risk losing the element of surprise, which I might need.

Tapping the unloaded gun against my leg, I blew out a breath and stepped into the pitch-black stairwell. I closed my eyes and told myself this was nothing like the closet they put me in back home, even if it smelled like it. Biting back the gut-churning response my body had to this place, I opened my eyes and climbed toward the next level.

The only promise of light crept in around the broken second level door, and I climbed faster despite my protesting muscles. It had been one helluva day, and it wasn't even noon yet.

My steps fell in place with my heartbeat, and I stopped to catch my breath on the landing. As I straightened, a cold tendril touched the back of my neck, and I shouted, stumbling out of the stairwell. I batted and smacked the possible remnants away as I spun around.

Loose wiring swung in the doorway. Loose wiring was what nearly gave me a heart attack. I wasn't sure how much more I could take. I officially needed to get out of the creepiest building I'd ever seen, before I lost my damn mind.

A clank and a scurry of footsteps echoed in the hall ahead, and my head whipped to the side.

"Hello," I said quietly, holding my breath as my voice ricocheted in the dimness. I didn't dare move as I strained to listen. "I heard someone crying—I just wanted to make sure you're all right." My voice was deep, but my chest heaved fast and hard. "I'm gonna go if you don't say something," I threatened.

Hushed voices drifted down the hall, and I heard the patter of feet again.

"Listen, kid." I was done trying to be the good guy. "If this is some idea of a joke, I swear to God—" My voice caught in my throat as a small girl peeked her head around the corner of the hall-way, her long hair catching in the breeze. I couldn't make out much in the shadows, but she looked around five or six years old, and scared. Her eyes shimmered with tears, but she seemed to be in one piece.

"What are you doing in here?" My stomach churned as it dawned on me that no one in their right mind would be out here playing, and definitely not alone. "Where—" I cleared my throat. "Where are your parents? You shouldn't be in here."

Wiping the tears from her eyes, the girl straightened and stepped into the hallway—fully into view.

"Don't—" a small voice chided behind her. "Thea!" An arm reached out to grab her, but she stepped out of the way and glanced back at him.

A boy a few years older than her stepped out into the open and reached hastily for her hand.

"I won't hurt you," I told them, holding my palms up.

"Then why do you have a gun?" the boy asked, pulling the little girl closer beside him.

"I'll tell you why I have a gun when you explain why you're up here, and why you're both crying." I glanced behind them, half-expecting someone or something else to be lurking, bearing fangs with wild, red eyes.

I studied the little girl, who was clearly more willing to speak than the boy was. "It's *Thea*, right? Are you in here alone?"

She started to nod, and the boy jerked her arm. Thea glared at him, like a little sister glares at an older brother, but he shook his head in warning.

"At least come back with me, out of the cold. You shouldn't be playing in here, you'll both get sick."

"We're not playing," Thea squeaked out.

"And we've already been sick," the boy added. Both of them sniffed, and Thea wiped at her eyes.

Taking a few slow steps forward, I tried to make out their features—to see their sincerity. The closer I drew, the more rigid they became, but they didn't run. When I was thirty feet away, I stopped. The gray morning light illuminated the skin beneath their eyes—red and raw from crying. They had on puffy coats, soiled pajama bottoms, snow boots, and their lips were chapped.

"Have you been sleeping here?" The thought of it nearly broke my heart, especially as pure sadness and exhaustion filled their eyes. "How long have you been out here?"

Thea shrugged and rubbed her eye with the palm of her hand again.

"Since last night," the boy explained. His voice was hoarse, either from fear or from sadness.

"Alone?"

Thea shook her head. "With Mommy."

I crouched down, feeling the cold cement of the floor seep through my boots. The boy's gaze fixed on the gun in my hand, and I shook my head. "It's not loaded." I tossed it aside to reassure them. "I wasn't sure what I'd find in here." I glanced between them. "Where is your mom now?"

While the boy was deciding what to say, Thea pointed behind her.

"Thea," he chided. "Stop it."

I clenched my jaw, restless to move things along and get the hell out of there. "I'm Alex," I told the little girl, since the boy seemed too skeptical to trust me. "I want to help. Your mommy, she's here in the building?"

The boy heaved out a sigh. "She fell."

"That's who I heard crying?" I jumped to my feet and took a

step toward them as the boy took a few steps back. "Look, I'm not going to hurt you," I said, holding up my hands again. I couldn't help the impatience in my voice. "But I need to help your mom. Don't you want me to help her? Take me to her—okay? It's the only way I can."

Thea hurried down the hallway, tugging her brother behind her. I fell into step behind them, uneasy as they began to slow at a room a few doors down before they disappeared inside. Reluctantly, I stepped inside behind them. It was an old office of sorts with an overturned desk in the corner and a moth-eaten blanket piled in the corner. The kids stopped in front of the far window. "Why are we in here?" There was no mother—crying, injured, or other.

Thea looked from me to the window and took a step away from it, like she was afraid of heights.

Confused, I inched closer and reluctantly looked down into the snow. A woman's form, twisted and broken, was partially covered with snow.

I spun around and looked between them. The little girl grabbed her brother's hand and they both eyed me warily. "She fell out the window?"

They looked at each other. "Yeah, she fell," the brother said.

"The bad men were coming," Thea explained. "She wanted to get away from the bad men."

The bad men? "What did they want?" The boy's hands were crusted with dry blood, and the dirt on their clothes looked more like streaks—like they'd been dragged. "Did they hurt you?" Something didn't feel right. When neither of them spoke, I took a slow step closer. "You won't be in trouble. Whatever happened last night, it's not your fault. I promise." I knew what it felt like to be scared of the truth. "But you have to tell me what happened. Where are the bad men?" If there was one thing I *could* do for these kids, it was to figure out a way to get them the help they needed.

Beau shrugged. "We didn't see them—"

"She tried to push Beau," Thea blurted. "But I didn't want her to." Her face crumpled and she began to cry again.

"You tried to save your brother?" I said, looking at the boy's size compared to her own, then out the window again, two stories down at the woman's body. Had she even fallen far enough to die on impact, or had she frozen to death after?

Strangely, her feet were bare and she looked like she was in nothing more than soiled pajamas. No sane person would be outside wearing next to nothing. "She tried to push you," I repeated, and I began to put the pieces together. I could understand their fear and imagine her in a craze. My gaze fixed on a dark blur on her wrist, and squinting, I gulped a lungful of air. A lotus tattoo was placed squarely on her wrist, and I felt sick to my stomach all over again.

"Mrs. Gunderson—" I looked at Thea and Beau. "Katie Gunderson is your mom—you're her sick kids?"

They blinked at me, their chins trembling as they watched me pace in a sudden panic. My teacher was dead—and she'd tried to kill her kids? While part of me couldn't believe it, the reversal made even less sense. No woman in her right mind would bring her sick kids out into an abandoned building without proper clothing in the middle of the night.

Their mom is dead.

Their dead mom is my teacher.

"Look," I said, squeezing my eyes shut as I realized this was some shitty shit I happened to stumble on. "We'll get it all sorted out, okay? We'll get you home." At least that part I could figure out. "You guys need to get warm, and we need to find your dad—" I frowned. "Where is your dad?"

Beau shrugged, and Thea blinked at me.

"We'll find someone to help—we'll find your dad, okay? We'll find help," I repeated more quietly, for myself this time.

Thea nodded, clearly happy to get out of the barracks; but once again, Beau hesitated. "What will they do to her?"

"To who?"

"Thea," he said.

"Kid, she's like, five. They won't do anything—they won't even believe it. *I* don't even believe it." I nodded down the hall. "Now, come on. This place is freaking me out."

I turned again, finally hearing the pitter-patter of footsteps behind me, and I headed back toward the stairwell. The kids whisper-argued back and forth, but I couldn't understand what they were saying. I was walking too fast, the adrenaline pumping too loud.

None of it made any sense—not the old man with his empty gun, not Thea being strong enough to push her mother out of a window, and not my teacher being crazy enough to hurt her own kids.

I'd never been so grateful to feel snow beneath my feet as we came out of the building. The wind raked over me, nearly making me stumble, but I would brave whatever I had to, to get back to Jimmy and his shitty-ass apartment.

Thea screeched as she tried to catch her scarf, flapping away in the wind. Her hair whipped around her face, and Beau ran after her scarf to no avail. It was nearly a mile back to the apartment complex, and as tall and close as it looked from where we stood, the kids had already been through enough.

I searched the parked vehicles scattered around the warehouse a hundred yards away. The Dodge was out of gas, and the only vehicle that looked like it might even start was an old Ford van, parked under an awning beside the warehouse.

I flipped my collar up around my ears, wishing I hadn't forgotten my beanie in the boat, and jogged over to the van.

"Come on!" I called to them, and was relieved the driver side door was unlocked when I reached it. Now, I just needed the damn thing to start. I searched around inside for the keys.

The passenger side door squeaked open. "Is this your car?" Beau asked, his nose and lips were pink with cold.

No," I told him, reaching under the dashboard to feel for the wiring. "But we're going to borrow it."

87

FIFTEEN
ALEX

Hot air hit me as we stepped through the side entrance into the apartment building. I blew a stray bit of snow from my cheek and peeked down the hall. The door swung shut behind us, bathing us in one last rush of frigid air before we were surrounded by sudden silence.

Unlike the moment I stomped out of the building to find a place to sleep, exhausted with my head throbbing, no one was rushing around or herding me out the door this time. The hissing vents were all I could hear, a strange sweet stench in the air was all I could smell.

I glanced over my shoulder at Thea and Beau. I'd been awake less than a couple of hours and there were two kids relying on me to help them. I just hoped that I could.

Certain we would find someone, *anyone* to help us, I peered down the hallway. "This is the direction everyone was going," I remembered aloud. It was where the signs pinned up on the walls pointed to as well, so we followed the arrows. All I needed was to find one adult. They'd know what to do with two orphaned kids. They might even know who their father was and where to find him. Everyone knew everyone in a place like this.

But the longer we walked in silence, the more certain I was that something was not right—no, not something, *nothing* was right. Not the fever I thought would kill me, or the kids hiding in an abandoned building, and not the dead man I'd found outside the warehouse, or my dead teacher.

At least the apartment complex was lit, and after stalking the abandoned hallways of the Heston Building, the connection tunnel to the classrooms and gymnasium felt less ominous than it had the first day of school.

"Hello?" The wind rushed outside the tunnel. I stopped where the hallway forked, right for the classrooms and left for the gym.

I looked back at Beau and Thea a few yards behind me. "I'm going to find someone, but stay here, okay?"

Beau's lips pursed, and his eyes shone with concern. "Don't leave," he said, taking a step closer.

"I'm not going far, okay? Just down here. You can see me the whole way." I peeled off my soiled jacket, growing too warm in the heat of the building. "I just need to see if there are people who can help us. If there aren't, I'll come right back. I promise." Even if I was all they had, it made me feel a little better that Beau had warmed to me, at least a little, like maybe, finally, he was starting to trust me.

"Look," I said, gesturing down the hall. The lights flickered, but there was no one in either direction. "No monsters. I'll be right back."

Finally, they both conceded, and leaned against the wall to wait for my return.

Letting out a deep breath, I peered back down the hall toward the gym. I didn't like how quiet everything was, not compared to what it had been, and though my instinct was to turn back, I walked closer. There was only one way to find help.

The further down the hall I walked, the more I noticed a trend. A couple of purses and backpacks were discarded in the corridor, as well as a lone tennis shoe. Things were hastily abandoned, but it was the fact they were *important* items, like shoes and purses, that worried me the most. I wasn't sure if it was my imagination, but the closer I drew to the gym, the stronger the sickly-sweet stench in the air became. It wasn't good, whatever it was. Every trembling nerve in my body told me as much.

I swallowed thickly as the gym doors came into view. "Hello, is anyone there—" I stopped a yard or so shy of the doorway, staring at five fingers attached to a half-closed hand lying over the threshold, the rest of the body out of view. I clenched my jaw so tight, my teeth ground together.

Whose hand was in the doorway, and what else would I find when I stepped closer?

I glanced frantically back at Thea and Beau. "Stay there," I reiterated with a harsh whisper. Whatever authority my voice held was enough, and Beau nodded, pulling his sister closer to him. My eyes were already burning from the acrid scent permeating the corridor, and I knew exactly where it was coming from.

Sucking in a breath, I inched closer. I didn't want to know what was inside, but some sick part of me needed to—to know what was in the gym.

"Hello?" Like ripping off a bandage, I forced myself to take four quick steps closer so I could see, and just as quickly, as I saw the flash of a gaping mouth and red-splattered body, I spun back around and heaved.

The sight. The scent. The utter disbelief. All of it came pouring out of me, wringing my stomach dry, every last bit of energy with it.

A flash was all I'd needed. Bodies were everywhere. On cots lined up against the walls, wrapped in blankets on the floor. Some bodies were sprawled out, others doubled over. All of them were deceased.

I gagged, spitting the bile from my mouth.

There were carts covered in bloodied rags. I could see the people in their pajamas and scrubs, street clothes and uniforms.

Women and men, children and babies. They all came here to die. And I gagged again.

The flu had come and gone, and these people hadn't made it. But there were others, like me and Beau and Thea, there had to be, and I stumbled back down the hallway toward them. The gymnasium was no longer a makeshift hospital, it was a crypt, and we had to find the other survivors.

"Beau," I called, clearing my throat. "Where do you live? We have to find your dad."

SIXTEEN
SOPHIE

The sound of an alarm made me jolt up in bed. "What?" I blinked, looking around, momentarily lost in the pale shadows of my room. "Mom?" I said, licking my lips. They were rough against my tongue, and it felt like I'd eaten handfuls of sand.

The high-pitched noise sounded from the living room again, and I startled awake even more.

"The following message is issued at the request of emergency management." A man's voice resonated through the house.

"Mom!" I called again, wishing she would turn the TV down. I flung my covers back and winced as I tried to climb out of bed. It felt like I'd been run over by a truck. Twice.

"Due to the possibility of a viral outbreak, a mandatory quarantine has been issued for all cities in Alaska with five hundred or more civilians."

I paused, my robe in hand, and listened as the man's words began to sink in.

"Alaska residents, including those in Juneau, Anchorage, and Fairbanks, are asked to stay tuned to television and radio stations for further updates."

I rushed out to the living room, nearly running into the arm of the couch.

White and bold, EMERGENCY ALERT SYSTEM flashed on the black screen of the TV. *A statewide quarantine?*

The EAS screen continued to flash in silence. "Mom, are you hearing this?" I fumbled to her bedroom, dread filling me when I saw her bed was made, and she wasn't in there. "Mom . . ." But she'd turned the TV on, right? Or had I? I remembered screaming and voices in my dreams. Had it been the TV?

I hurried back to the couch and reached for my phone sticking out from between the couch cushions. Only five percent battery life. I barely cared. I dialed my mom's cell as the crazed night came flooding back to me.

"Mom, answer the phone!" I yelled. I pulled my phone from my ear and stared at the clock dumbly.

Two days—I'd been out for two days! I heard my mom's voice in my phone speaker. "Mom—" I held it to my ear again.

"—Tessa Collins. Please leave me a message, and I will return your call at my earliest convenience. If this is about the upcoming election, please call my work phone at 342-3493. Thank you." The message beeped, but all I could do was breathe into the void.

Quarantine. The word was jarring, though I wasn't sure why. Of course, it made sense. JJ was coughing up blood. She couldn't breathe.

If things were as bad as I thought they were, the news had to be reporting about it somewhere. I dropped my cell phone and clicked the remote to pull up CNN, but every single channel was the same—black.

The EAS signal beeped again, and the white letters continued to flash on the screen. EMERGENCY ALERT SYSTEM.

"The civil authorities have issued a civil emergency message beginning at 4:05 p.m. The following message is issued at the request of the governor of the state of Alaska. This is not a test. The State of Alaska is declaring an official ban on all trade and commerce. All travel is restricted to minimize the spread of the infectious disease. Effective immediately, the Coast Guard will patrol all ports and harbors, airports, and railways to enforce this ban. State troopers will patrol the streets to ensure everyone conducts themselves in an orderly manner."

The hole in my stomach grew, and I picked up my phone to dial my mom's work number this time. I sighed when it wasn't busy, and sat down on the couch, allowing myself to calm down long enough to catch my breath. But as the phone continued to ring, the nothingness inside my stomach began to churn again. "Pick up," I pleaded, tears filling my eyes.

I dialed her number again. No answer. Then dialed again, knowing she might not be at her desk, but if she heard her phone ring from wherever she was, she would pick it up . . . if she could. "Please pick—"

"Jenny, it's Elle!" A voice echoed in the hallway. "Is anyone in there? I'm looking for my sister, Jenny St. James." I could hear a woman pounding a few doors down. "Jenny, it's me." Desperation filled her voice as she drew closer, banging and calling to no avail.

I ran to the door to peek out the peephole. I couldn't see her. "Somebody . . . Hello!" A gut-wrenching sob filled the hallway, and I rested my forehead against the door, uncertain if I should open it. A quarantine meant things were bad. She might have been infected, but I was desperate to know what was happening out there. I was desperate to talk to someone.

"Hello," the woman sobbed, as the hope drained from her voice.

If she'd been downstairs, she could tell me what was happening. Biting my lip, I squeezed the tears from my eyes and shook my head, praying I wouldn't regret opening the door.

Reluctantly, I unlocked it. Even if I was going to make a run for the elevator to get downstairs, I would have to see her. But when I cracked the door open, the hallway was quiet.

I opened the door further, and poked my head out.

"Hello?" she whispered. She was braced against the wall a dozen yards to the right, cheeks red as she wiped the tears from her wide eyes. Her snow jacket and beanie were discarded on the carpet, and she clasped her gloved hands together. "Oh, thank God." She ran toward me, and the gun in her belt flashed in the overhead lights. Barely containing a shriek, I slammed the door shut again, and locked it.

"No!" she shouted.

Stupid. Stupid—stupid *Sophie.*

"Please—please don't shut the door." The woman banged on the other side, rattling my head against the door as I leaned back, silently pleading she'd go away.

I covered my face with my hand to stifle my cries.

"I need to find my sister. She lives on this floor—Jenny St. James. Please—you're the only person I've seen."

She knocked again, only this time, my breath caught in my throat. The only person she'd seen?

"Do you know her? She's my twin—she looks just like me." Her pounding ceased, and I heard a thud against the door. "Please," she whispered. "I need your help."

She hadn't seen *anyone* else?

Wiping the tears from my eyes, perhaps to appear stronger than I was, I slid the chain lock into place and creaked the door open a crack.

"Oh, thank you—thank you!" The woman was right; she was JJ's twin, though she was very much alive compared to her sister. "Do you know where Jenny lives?"

"JJ lived there," I rasped, and nodded next door.

Her twin didn't skip a beat as she rushed toward the apartment and disappeared inside.

Ten minutes and three glasses of water later, I was dressed in a sweatshirt and my pajama shorts, which was about all I could manage in the heat of the building. I was unable to resist the idea of going next door. JJ's sister was still in there, and I needed to know what she'd learned downstairs.

Head aching and arms weak, I opened the front door and peeked my head out. JJ's apartment door was still open, and I could hear footsteps echoing on the tile kitchen floor. Arms wrapped around myself, I crept down the hall, still uncertain I trusted the woman at all, and after a dozen or so yards, I stopped in the doorway of JJ's apartment, and peered in.

Her twin stood in the kitchen, staring at a photo in her hand. I'd seen twins before, but not identical ones in person. They were so similar and so very different at the same time. JJ's hair was long, nearly down to her waist, but her sister's hung just past her shoulders. JJ wore all black most of the time, but her sister looked more like a college student come home for the holidays. She seemed younger somehow too.

The floor creaked beneath my feet, and she looked at me. Her eyes were sad, and dark circles shadowed them. I knew the feeling.

She held up the photo of her sister. "Do you know where she is?"

I blinked at her, uncertain what to say, and in my hesitation, she stepped closer.

"Have you seen my sister or not?" Her nostrils flared, and her voice was thick with fear.

Her sister was dead, I'd seen her name crossed out on the clipboard, but I didn't know how to tell her; all I could do was nod. "They took her away on a stretcher."

She straightened and her eyebrows drew together. I wasn't sure if it was sadness or resolve that filled her green eyes. "To quarantine?"

"I don't know." I had no idea if she'd made it that far or not.

"You don't know? Did she go to quarantine or not?"

"I don't know!" I barked back, and wiped my nose with my sleeve. "I never saw her again. My mom told me to stay upstairs and not open the door or leave this floor—she made me swear." It was a plea, a frantic screech, because the truth was I had no idea what happened to her sister, just that she was dying the last time I saw her, and I couldn't imagine someone coming back from that.

A resigned defeat dimmed the woman's eyes, and she nodded.

It was as if she'd already known. "Where did your mom go?"

I shook my head and threw my hands up. "She was helping the people from the cruise ship on the first floor. I've been calling her, but she hasn't answered."

This time, her eyes widened with surprise. "She's the mayor."

How could she know? I stepped closer, my legs already shaking from both weakness and fear, but I dared to hope. "Have you seen her?"

With an all too familiar reluctance, she nodded. Her steadying deep breath said it all.

Tears, hot and burning in the backs of my eyes, filled my vision. "She's dead?" I croaked. The sympathy in her gaze barely registered as I choked out a sob. "My mom's dead?"

A cloud of despair settled over me in her silence. "She's dead . . ." I wasn't sure I'd even spoken the words as every part of me began to unravel. My mom couldn't be dead. She was going to come home when everything was fixed.

I doubled over, gasping for breath as another body-wracking sob came over me. I didn't get to tell her how much I loved her—I didn't get to say goodbye.

The woman wrapped her arms around me and pulled me against her, her body trembling with quiet sobs. I grabbed hold of her shirt as a cancerous melody of fear, regret, and sadness consumed me.

My mom was dead. I would never see her again, ever. And I was alone.

SEVENTEEN
ALEX

We checked the tourism office on the first floor, hoping Beau and Thea's dad would be at his desk, but he wasn't. I made the kids stay near the broom closet while I checked the video rental shop and market. The market was trashed, completely raided, and I assumed it was to feed the gym full of people who hadn't made it.

Desperate to find someone besides us, we opted to take the stairs up to Jimmy's apartment, one floor below the Gundersons. The blood splattered elevator wasn't something I thought I could handle after what I'd seen in the gym, and I tried to push it from my mind.

Jimmy wasn't there, but his apartment was destroyed. Everything was upturned and broken, including the window. Even if I knew in my gut that I'd find him eight stories below, I had to check —just to know for sure. I got close enough to lean through the shattered glass and peered down at the third body I'd seen today, half covered in snow. Unlike Mrs. Gunderson, Jimmy's outline was so far down I couldn't be entirely certain it was him. I felt guilty not caring much that he was dead, only that he couldn't help me.

Forcing myself once again to focus, I changed into fresh clothes that didn't smell like I'd shit myself, and as quickly as I could, I ushered the kids back out to look for their dad. My hope to find him was depleted though, and I did all I could to hold myself together.

They needed someone, and unfortunately for them, I was all they had at the moment. I needed to be strong, for now at least. I had to do this *for them*.

When we reached their apartment, I knocked on the door. The last thing I needed was someone to shoot me, thinking I was sick. "Mr.—uh—Gunderson? Are you in there? I have Beau and Thea out here with me."

I glanced down at them; both of their brows etched with hope and worry as they stared at the door, willing it to open. I jiggled the handle, uncertain if I was relieved to find it unlocked, or petrified.

"You guys should stay here until I say it's okay. All right? We don't know what's inside."

Thea and Beau had been so strong, but the anticipation was too much, and as their expressions began to crumble, their voices broke, and they began to cry.

"Dad!" Beau called, and tears filled my eyes. "Are you in there, Daddy?"

Thea wiped at her eyes with little shaking hands, and I knew I needed to get this over with.

Clenching my jaw, I crouched down, my vision blurring with tears of my own. "I know you're scared," I told them as delicately as I could. "But you have to stay here, okay? We have to make sure your dad isn't going to hurt you." *Like your mom did.*

That was all Beau needed to hear, and he nodded and licked the tears from his lips.

I pointed to the wall. "Stand back over there until I say it's safe." I wasn't sure having them see their father dead from the virus or not there at all was better or worse.

They leaned against the wall and slid down to sit beside one another and wait. I stared up at the ceiling. *Please . . . Please let him be alive so they have* someone *left*. A clawing sense of desperation to not be the one person they'd have left to rely on made it difficult to step inside.

When I opened the door, there was no more gray light of day, only lamplight from the side tables in the living room. It was sparsely decorated with a futon couch and a bookshelf in the corner, lined with plastic horse figurines and G.I. Joes. A fish tank was lit in the back corner by the window, and a large flat screen TV hung on the far wall.

The apartment smelled like maple syrup and dish soap, and the kitchen was cluttered with a few dirty dishes in the sink. Hand-drawn artwork was stuck to the fridge, and a large chore calendar hung on the wall between the counter and the refrigerator, golden stars filling nearly every day.

I had a fifty-fifty chance their dad was here and not in the gym, likely dead given the silence, and I had three rooms to figure it out. Wanting to get it over with, I poked my head into the first room, knowing instantly it was Thea's. Her pink bedspread was pulled back and a barf bowl, filled with vomit that reeked as it hit my nostrils, sat on the beige carpet beside it. Like the rest of the building, their apartment was sweltering hot, and I nearly gagged as I pulled the door shut.

Blinking the burn from my eyes, I turned to the next room. It was Beau's, and the walls were cluttered with sports posters, and Army figurines scattered across the floor.

The power flickered on and off, and I stared up at the hall light, praying it would give me a few seconds longer. There was one last room to check, and I clung to all the willpower that remained as I nudged open the final bedroom door.

There was no body on the unmade bed. I swallowed thickly and stepped further in. I didn't see a body on the floor, either. But there was blood, almost like footprints in a chaotic pattern near the mirrored closet door. I saw a flash of red in the bathroom and squeezed my fist closed.

Trying not to prolong the inevitable, I strode over and peered into the bathroom. I swallowed thickly. Shards of glass covered the ground, blood pooled and streaked against the white laminate, and the entire mirror was smashed to pieces.

Vomit and blood. Why did it have to be vomit *and* blood? I pushed thoughts of my mother away as the lights flickered again.

There was no body, and as every bloody memory I ever had came blaring back to life, it pushed me too far to the edge, and I fell backward.

The day I found my mother had been the day everything changed—the day I lost the one person who I'd wanted to love me unconditionally to an overdose or suicide, whichever it had been. Regardless, I'd meant nothing to her, definitely not as much as *him*. My sister was gone, my grandma and horrible uncle were gone too. My entire existence felt tainted. I was discarded. I was alone.

I didn't know what happened to Mr. Gunderson, but I knew it was something awful, and I couldn't stay in the apartment a second longer.

"He's not here," I called, rushing out the door. "He's not here, and we have to go."

"Where are we going?" Thea huffed, and she sniffled behind me. "Where's my daddy?"

I shook my head because I had no idea. I didn't know where we were going or where their father was, but I needed air.

I smacked my hand against the elevator button, praying it still worked. I had no idea what had happened inside, but there was more blood than I was comfortable with, and the three of us opted for the stairs up, until now.

The elevator button glowed red when I pushed it, but it wouldn't come fast enough. I needed to know if we were the only ones left, and the tenth floor was my last hope.

Finally, the doors opened, and I ignored the splatter marring the elevator walls; it was easier this time after what I'd seen in the bathroom, only minimal in comparison.

Beau and Thea hurried in behind me. "Come on, Thea," Beau quipped. "Keep up. And close your eyes."

As the elevator doors dinged to close us inside, I stared at the buttons. *The tenth floor.* "Sophie," I breathed. She was the only other person I knew. I leaned my head against the elevator door and squeezed my eyes shut as I pressed the button for the last apartment floor. I didn't know what I would do if she wasn't there —or if I found her dead too.

Please be alive. I let the tears drip from my eyes and splash onto the elevator floor. *Please be alive.*

"Alex . . ." Thea whispered.

"I just—I need a minute of silence, okay?" I told them, trying to keep my calm. "I need to think." The bodies in the gymnasium. The scent of death. The blood. I needed it to be a dream. I needed it all to be a horrible dream.

If Sophie was dead too, we'd have to leave. We'd go some-where, we'd stay off the grid until we knew what was going on— I'd figure something out. I tried to ignore the practical questions, like where we would go and how we would get there. I might've been a delinquent teen in the court's eyes, but I was resourceful if nothing else. I'd figure it out. I always did. But I could use a teensy-weensy break.

The elevator doors opened, and Beau and Thea blinked at me, waiting for me to lead the way. Forcing myself to keep it together —telling myself I couldn't help Kayla but I could help them—I wiped the tears from my eyes with my long sleeve and nodded. "Let's go."

The three of us stepped into the hallway, but I didn't know which apartment was Sophie's or which way to go.

I peered to the right and the left, hating that I always had to choose a damn hallway; there was never anything good on either side. I noticed two open doorways at the end of the right wing, and slowly, I started toward them.

Please be alive. Please be alive. Please *be alive . . .*

Beau and Thea's footsteps were quiet behind mine, and they were likely holding their breath, like I was. Their jackets whooshed in the silence as they brushed against one another, and I was acutely aware of the breakdown I would likely have once I discovered the kids and I were all that was truly left in this place.

We hadn't taken a dozen steps before I heard someone crying inside one of the apartments. I froze. Licked my lips. Dared to hope. And I dragged in a breath. "Sophie?" My voice was firm and more certain than I felt in the quiet hall, but the soft mewing cries stopped. I held my breath.

Thea slid her hand into mine, and I peered down at her. Her eyes were glued to the open doorway as she squeezed my hand.

I squeezed hers back gently, grateful to have the two kids, at least. When I glanced up, Sophie stood like an angel on the threshold, her face swollen and red with grief. And she was frowning at me.

"Alex?" All I could do was stare at her, blinking and praying she was real. She took a step closer and her chest began to heave. Her lips moved, like maybe she wanted to say something, but her eyes clouded with tears as she began to walk closer. "I thought everyone was dead."

"Me too." I thought I might've laughed with relief, but it was a sob, and in that moment Sophie ran toward me.

Her arms were around my neck, clutching hold of me. "I can't believe you're alive," she cried into my chest.

Faintly, a distant voice told me I shouldn't be so relieved she was alive, I barely knew her. And yet, relief was all I could feel —and comfort that I wasn't alone. It was more intense than I thought possible, more desperate, like the reassurance of her and I combined was humming through me, and it was all I could feel.

I tried to say something, but my voice caught in my throat. Closing my eyes, I inhaled the scent of her. She didn't smell like clean linen anymore, but she was real and breathing. I tightened my arms around her, relishing the feel of a warm body. A familiar face. A living person.

"I'm really glad to see you." My words were barely a breath— a ragged inhale and clipped sob. I'd never been so happy to see anyone in my entire life, and in that moment, it felt like everything might actually be okay.

With a sniffle, Sophie pulled away, and with her went my heightened sense of relief, like it retreated with the warmth of her body as she took a step back.

I cleared my throat and wiped my eyes, remembering Beau and Thea standing uncertain behind me. "When I saw the blood in the elevator," I started, but Sophie quickly shook her head.

"It's JJ's."

I frowned, uncertain who that was, just overwhelmingly glad it wasn't Sophie's.

"Her sister came to find her." She glanced at the apartment door at the end of the hall. The sympathy on Sophie's face, and the blood on the carpet and in the elevator, explained the rest.

"It's just the five of us then," I said.

Sophie dipped her head. "Yeah." Her voice was so quiet I barely heard the word, and she glanced up at me with glistening blue eyes. I wasn't sure what the past couple of days had been like for her, but if they were remotely like mine, it was as close as she'd probably been to hell.

"For now," I added, more reassuring than certain, and I squared my shoulders and took a deep breath. "We'll figure this out."

Whether Sophie believed me or just hoped it was true, she seemed to cling to the words and pursed her lips with a nod, trying to be strong. "We'll figure this out," she repeated. "Together."

THE END

I hope you enjoyed Alex and Sophie's origin story! Have you read *The Darkest Winter*, the first book in the series? It's over 500 pages of survival and adventure as six strangers face the horrors of a virus-ravaged world, and the hope, love, and family they find in one another along the way. And find out what happens next with Alex, Sophie, and the gang in *Midnight Sun*.

Audiobooks, ebook, and signed paperbacks are available in my bookshop (and all major retailers).

You can find more information on my website www.lindseypogue.com

OTHER BOOKS BY LINDSEY

FORGOTTEN WORLD

(Stand-alones, suggested reading order)

RUINED LANDS

City of Ruin

Sea of Storms

Land of Fury

FORGOTTEN LANDS

Dust and Shadow

Borne of Sand and Scorn Prequel Novella

Earth and Ember

Tide and Tempest

THE ENDING WORLD

SAVAGE NORTH CHRONICLES

(Reading order)

The Darkest Winter

The Longest Night

Midnight Sun

Fading Shadows

Untamed

Unbroken

Day Zero: Beginnings

THE ENDING SERIES

After The Ending

Into The Fire

Out Of The Ashes

Before The Dawn

The Ending Beginnings

World Before

THE ENDING LEGACY

World After

The Raven Queen

For behind-the-scene access to exclusive projects, check out my VIP reader community.

ABOUT LINDSEY POGUE

Lindsey Pogue is a genre-bending fiction author, best known for her soul-stirring survival adventures and timeless love stories. As an avid romance reader with a master's in history and culture, Lindsey's series cross genres and push boundaries, weaving together facts, fantasy, and romance set in rich, sweeping land-scapes of epic proportions. When she's not chatting with readers, plotting her next storyline, or dreaming up new, brooding characters, Lindsey's generally wrapped in blankets watching her favorite action flicks with her own leading man. They live in Northern California with their rescue cats, Beast and Blue.

For newsletter signups, memberships, exclusive content, and bookshop discounts, visit the Savage North Hub.